The
Runaways

A REBA **2** NOVEL

The Runaways

Marian Flandrick Bray

ZondervanPublishingHouse
Grand Rapids, Michigan
A Division of HarperCollins*Publishers*

The Runaways
Copyright © 1992 by Marian Bray

Requests for information should be addressed to:
Zondervan Publishing House
Grand Rapids, Michigan 49530

Library of Congress Cataloging-in-Publication Data

Bray, Marian Flandrick, 1957–
    The runaways / by Marian Bray.
      p. cm.
    Summary: When she learns that her mother plans to remarry, Reba and her pet burro run away to the mountains.
    ISBN 0-310-54361-4 (pbk.)
    [1. Runaways—Fiction. 2. Donkeys—Fiction. 3. Remarriage—Fiction.] I. Title.
PZ7.B7388Ru   1992
[Fic]—dc20   92–11449
                                                    CIP
                                                    AC

Edited by Dave Lambert
Interior designed by Louise Bauer
Cover designed by Gary Gnidovic
Cover illustration by Matthew Archambault

Printed in the United States of America

92 93 94 95 96 / AK / 10 9 8 7 6 5 4 3 2 1

To:
Stacie Johnson,
our summer kid,
and
Maury Aaseng,
an animal lover, too

Many thanks to Ranelda Hunsicker for helping me with the secrets in this book.

Appreciation to the Angeles Girl Scout Council for all the fun treks into the San Gabriel Mountains and overnights at Camp Bon Accord.

Also to Wolfgang, my faithful canine companion, for hiking with me in the San Gabriels—and for only throwing up once in the car on the mountain roads.

Contents

Then a great and powerful wind tore the mountains apart and shattered the rocks before the Lord, but the Lord was not in the wind. After the wind there was an earthquake, but the Lord was not in the earthquake. After the earthquake came a fire, but the Lord was not in the fire. And after the fire came a gentle whisper. When Elijah heard it, he pulled his cloak over his face and went out and stood at the mouth of the cave. Then a voice said to him, "What are you doing here, Elijah?"

—1 Kings 19:11–13

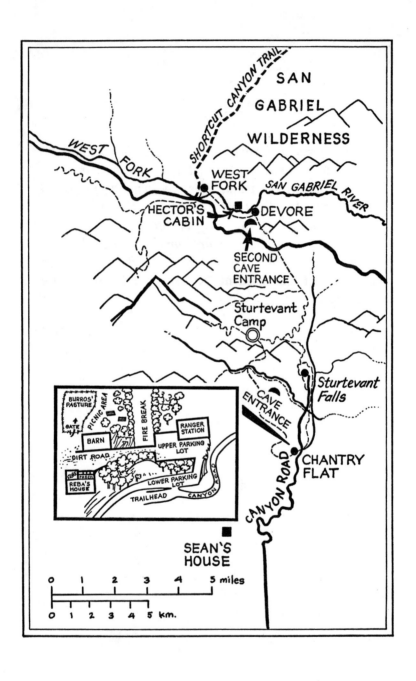

1
The Magic of the Mountains

I think it's time to run away," I said to Burrito, my baby burro. We walked down a thin, seldom-used mountain trail. Burrito was four months short of being one year old; I would be thirteen in three months. But really, we were equal in age—both of us were eager to leave our elders. For him, that meant his sire and the other grown-up burros. For me, that meant my mother and her boyfriend, soon to be her husband and my stepfather, Francisco.

"Time to run," I said again.

Burrito twitched his ears and didn't look impressed with the idea. But if he knew what I knew, he'd want to leave immediately.

The San Gabriel mountains baked under the southern California sun. Many plants were dying; some had already died. The little rain that fell a couple of months ago—our last—helped the living, but it also caused small mud slides that oozed down slopes not protected by living plants.

I stopped in some shade from a thick-branched manzanita bush and let the cool breeze slip by me. Burrito halted and lowered his head, swishing his pale, butterscotch-colored tail. He explored the ground for a snack. I wiped my bangs back and wondered what it would really be like to live up here. Live up here forever.

I knew the mountains better than I knew myself. And I just couldn't stay home anymore. Home was changing, like the winter fur shedding off wolves, from a beautiful silver to black.

"Let's go on," I said to Burrito and we moved out of the shadow into the sunlight, continuing along the ridge above the lower canyon trail. Burrito followed me like a big dog. Uncle Hector, who wasn't really my uncle but we all called him that, said Burrito was special. Of course, I thought he was special. But Uncle Hector insisted that white burros were magical.

Once at Uncle Hector's cabin we had talked about that. "Magic?" I had said. "I thought you believed in God. How can you believe in magic?"

Uncle Hector, wiry and brown like the mountains, deftly repaired a broken leather bridle. His Medicine Hat horse liked to catch the headstall on a branch and haul back, snapping the leather. "God and magic can't go together?" he asked. He was teasing me.

"No," I said scornfully.

Uncle Hector raised a black eyebrow and said, "Magic is *from* God." I thought he was still teasing me, but he wouldn't say any more about magic on that trip, even though I asked.

I ran up the gentle incline along the rocky side of a hill into a patch of oak trees, with Burrito trotting after me.

"Uncle Hector says oak trees are magic, too," I said. "The California Indians thought so." I was part Indian, from the Gabrielino tribe. My real father's great grandmother was a Gabrielino.

Burrito ate grass in the little patches of sunlight filtering through the leaves. "If you eat some of the magic trees, Burrito, you will get some magic, too, no?" But then God could sprinkle magic on us if he wanted.

I patted Burrito. He just nuzzled me out of his way and grazed on. I sat on the dirt in the shade again, enjoying the coolness. It had been so hot for months! And even when it did get cold at night, it stayed dry. The drought had been going on for five years now.

A couple of months ago, when the rain had fallen, I had been praying for rain—and then, like magic, it had rained. Maybe my prayer had helped God with the magic of rain. A lovely silver feeling ran through me, thinking I was helping God.

Burrito snuffled loudly. He was growing up fast. Soon he'd pass me up; he would be grown up before I was an adult. I put my head on my knees. *But I might not see him grown up.* Tears threatened, but I choked them back.

That was one of the bad things about Mama getting married to Francisco: They planned to move. Soon. That meant me and my three brothers would go with them, but not the burros. We'd be going away from the San Gabriel Mountains to a city called Santa Ana. Francisco kept telling me, "Reba, Santa Ana is only an hour away. Not the other side of the moon."

Big deal, I wanted to say. *Are you going to drive me back here every day because I want to be here in the San Gabriels, not there in Santa Ana? Not hardly.*

And I couldn't take Burrito with me because there would be no place for him, and because we were selling our pack station; the burros were being sold to a pack outfit in the Sierras.

But Burrito is mine. And I am his. We couldn't leave each other. And I can't leave the mountains, either. They're part of me.

Long, curved eucalyptus leaves rolled sideways in the wind. Years and years ago, someone planted a wind screen here with eucalyptus saplings imported all the way from Australia; eucalyptus trees aren't indigenous to the San Gabriel mountains.

Indigenous. Sean's new word. He has a calendar with a new word each day, and *indigenous* was one of them. It means that something is found in a place naturally, that it belongs there, like coyotes are *indigenous* to the mountains.

But if I went to live in Santa Ana, I'd be like the eucalyptus tree. I wouldn't belong. I'm indigenous to the mountains, not the city.

I sighed so loud that a crow flew straight up from a

branch overhead and flew away, cawing his annoyance.

Burrito moved around the small shady area, eating whatever grass had dared to raise itself from the dry, rumpled ground—rumpled because a mud slide had happened here. The dirt down the hill was bunched up on the trail like someone had melted tons of chocolate and poured it down the slope. A couple of thin, bent pine saplings were half buried in dirt, and a cluster of sturdy bushes had been pushed over by the slide.

Burrito's teeth clicked as he bit off grass. The cool breeze fanned around me, and I lifted my face toward it. The greasewood and manzanita bushes in front of me rustled like there was an animal in them, moving around. Then I noticed something odd. Above us, the trees had quit blowing. The leaves were perfectly still. Yet a wind, cool and moist smelling, did blow over me, softly turning the lower leaves of the half-buried bushes.

I got up suddenly. Burrito stared over his moonlight-colored shoulder at me. I stepped across the trail until I was directly in front of the gently-blowing bushes and crouched down. Sweat trickled along my backbone from the hot sun, but the breeze whispered in my face. Not continuously, but off and on, like something breathing. My heart kicked in my chest. A huge animal?

Slowly I parted the branches; dirt rained down on my head and hands. My heart pounded so hard that I nearly choked.

No animal peered back at me. Instead, a dark opening yawned.

2
Never Friends with You

That night in the kitchen on the phone with Sean, who is my best friend, I told him about the cave. "It looked big," I said. I turned my back, so my voice wouldn't carry into the living room where Mama and Francisco sat with the radio on, the pack station account books in front of them. "I only went a little way in because it got too dark." I had been afraid to go deep without a light.

"Did you have to crawl?" asked Sean. I could imagine him, in his own kitchen, sitting on the tile counter below the matching blue cabinets, the gold rim of his glasses gleaming in the light.

"No, I could stand up in it," I said. After I had pushed through the bushes, I'd cautiously stood in the cool, breathing darkness, stunned. A cave!

"Tomorrow I have to go to the orthodontist," Sean was saying. "But I can come over on Saturday, okay?"

"Okay. Bring a flashlight," I added.

I hung up the phone and stood on our worn linoleum floor, curling my toes with pleasure. A real cave. Oh sure, there were old mine shafts scattered around the mountains, left over from the gold-and-silver mining rush seventy, eighty years ago. But why hadn't anyone mentioned a cave before? The answer chilled me more than standing in the cave opening: because no one knew!

"Reba," called Francisco, suddenly.

He filled the kitchen doorway, tall, dark, his belly poking out like Burrito's dam's belly had before Burrito was born. Mama called it his beer belly and would pat it affectionately. Yick.

"Come with me to get Pio," said Francisco. Pio was my oldest brother. Yesterday Pio's car had croaked. He had a night class on Tuesdays and Thursdays at the local junior college. The bus line didn't run after nine.

"I've got—"

Francisco interrupted me. Now if I'd interrupted him, I'd be in trouble. "I know you've done all your homework," he said. "You said so at dinner."

I kept my mouth shut, but narrowed my eyes. *Well, if you know so much.*

Silently I got my sweatshirt from my room while

Mama gave me dagger looks from the couch. She had said to me earlier in the week, "What is with you? Your brothers are happy I'm getting married again. But it's not Francisco, is it? No man would be good enough for you."

My own father would be just fine, thank you.

Francisco and I went silently outside. He opened the passenger side of the truck and I climbed in. We roared out of the pack station parking lot and on down the mountain.

On either side of the road, the winds tossed the trees back and forth like a kid playing catch. Francisco drove quickly, neatly taking each curve. *He should,* I thought sourly. *He's visited us enough times to drive it blindfolded.*

We raced off the mountain, past Santa Anita Racetrack. Someday I'd like to work backside with the Thoroughbred horses. My Aunt Kate says that you have to be sixteen to exercise the horses on the track. She ought to know; she's ridden horses most of her life.

We headed west for Pasadena Community College. Pio wants to teach anthropology, specializing in Indians—especially California Indians, since our family comes from the Gabrielino tribe.

"No one in my family has ever gotten a college degree," commented Francisco as car headlights pierced the space between us.

"Not even you?" I couldn't help sounding surprised. He owned a bunch of Mexican restaurants; somehow I'd assumed that he had a fancy business degree.

"Nah," he said and glanced over at me with a smile. "But someday I would like to go back." There was a wistfulness in his voice that I didn't want to hear. I didn't want anything to break my resolve against him.

I looked out the window and said, "My aunt goes to CalTech."

"I know. She's a very bright girl."

Aunt Kate, really my cousin, is ten years older than me so I call her aunt. She's smart in math. She loves not just horses but all animals, like I do, and when she visits us she always insists on seeing the burros, especially Burrito. She even kisses him on his soft nose.

When she was my age, she used to run with a gang. She has a tattoo of a wolf head on her shoulder. But she's changed.

"What do you want to be when you grow up, Reba?" Francisco asked me. Even after knowing me a year or so, he still asked the stock kid questions that adults ask when they don't know what to say: How's school? What are you taking? Do you like your teacher? Blah, blah, blah.

I hated that question in particular: What do you want to be? Because I really, really didn't know. But I wasn't going to tell Francisco that.

"Oh, probably a vet," I said, airily. I knew I'd never be a vet, though, because I'd never make it through vet school. I was lousy in math. Besides, I wanted to have animals of my own, not take care of someone else's animals.

It seemed everyone knew what they wanted to do except me. Pio and his Indian passion. Miguel, my second-oldest brother, who was in ninth grade, wanted to build houses. Even my youngest brother, Andres, wanted to be a paramedic—not a fireman, but a paramedic. Sean wanted to be a philosopher, which made his psychologist mother have fits. But me—I just wanted to stay in the mountains forever.

But now with Mama and Francisco planning to move us off the mountain, what was I to do? And they expected me to be happy about that? I sighed.

We drove into Pasadena. The streets were bright with neon business signs, orange fog lights, and car headlights and taillights, cheerfully winking. A year ago, a big earthquake crumpled some buildings in Pasadena, but now the streets were tidy and clean again.

The college campus glowed. Cars were pulling out of parking lots; college kids thronged the sidewalks. Francisco pulled into a parking lot near a wide lawn and killed the engine.

"I wish you wouldn't be so upset about this all, Reba," said Francisco. He glanced over at me, his soft face like a sad dog's. "I just want us to be friends."

Friends! I went rigid in the front seat. He was taking me away from everything I loved. The mountains, the burros, my home, my best friend, Sean.

The cave. That was the answer. I'd run away. To the cave. The ultimate hideaway. Then I wouldn't have to listen to Francisco ever again, and no one would steal me away from the mountains and Burrito.

My brother crossed the parking lot from a four-story building, a girl walking beside him.

"Friends, Reba," pressed Francisco. "Please?" His eyes begged me and he reached his hand to touch me. I leaned away, the door handle digging into my ribs. I didn't answer Francisco. I couldn't, I just couldn't agree.

Francisco's gaze touched mine, then he stiffened, knowing without words. I turned my head away, ashamed, but stubborn.

Pio's voice reached us, muffled and laughing. The passenger door opened and Pio's voice came clear. "Hey, everyone, hi. Do you mind taking Jessica home, Francisco?"

"I'll get in the back," I said, never so helpful in my life, and I clambered over the seat to the small storage space between the front seat and the truck bed.

"No problem, Pio. Hi, Jessica," said Francisco. Jessica and I greeted each other as Francisco started the engine. As he pulled out of the parking lot, he glanced at me in the rearview mirror, but I busied myself leaning forward and talking to Jessica.

3
Beginning of a Long Weekend

On Friday afternoon, the bus doors whooshed open and I jumped down the steps. I waved to the bus driver and he waved back, turned the lumbering bus around in the lower parking lot, and headed down the hill in a cloud of exhaust.

Overhead, a cluster of crows screamed and whirled by. Uncle Hector told me that crows took good care of their families and that we people should be more like crows. I think he was talking about Papa, but

I'm not sure. I took a shortcut through the wooded embankment and headed for the pack station.

Even though it was Friday—no school for two days—I wasn't glad. Friday meant a weekend of Francisco, of listening to him complaining about the pack station and about how things would be different and better in Santa Ana. At least his truck wasn't here yet. Generally he came up late Friday, after supervising his restaurants.

I let the front screen door bang behind me. Mama was in the kitchen.

"Hi," I called and dumped my books on the round kitchen table.

She smiled up at me as she pushed tortilla dough. "How was school?"

I shrugged and sat on the phone stool. "Okay, I guess. We have to write a term paper. Ten pages long."

Mama's brow crinkled. "That's a long paper to write."

I nodded vigorously. She handed me a fresh-cooked tortilla, still warm. I rolled it up and ate it like a sausage.

"What will you write about?" she asked, wisps of her hair curling down her cheek.

"Packing burros and trailing with them." I hadn't known until I said it that that's what I was going to write about, but yeah, that's the only thing I *could* write ten pages about. Except for maybe God and the mountains and the philosophical stuff Sean and I talk about. But if I did that, my teacher would probably have a cow.

Mama stopped kneading the dough. "Reba, we have to move. You know that. We—"

Lecture number forty-five was coming. I jumped off the stool, my mouth full. "I'll go clean the stable, okay?" I managed to say. Mama sighed and nodded.

In the barn I hastily scooped donkey droppings. We called them D & D. Almost as potent as T-N-T. Burrito came down off the hill from the nearby pasture and brayed mournfully from the gate. I let him out and he wandered into the barn, snuffling at the wheelbarrow of poop.

"You scatologist," I told him fondly. A scatologist was a scientist who studied poop. Burrito could easily get a Ph.D. in poop.

"Let's go see that cave again, Burrito," I said, rolling the r's up and down the scale. Burrito gave me a bored look. I sang a little song, making it up as I went, about Bur*rrrrr*ito who ate the bur*rrrrr*ito at Francisco's *rrrrrr*estaurant.

Burrito, looking unimpressed, ambled over to the closed feed bin. He gave another harsh bray.

"No," I said, "you'll spoil your supper."

"Reba! Phone for you." Mama's voice whirled into the barn.

I carefully hung up the rake so Burrito wouldn't trip over it and ran back to the house. I picked up the phone in Mama's bedroom.

A pair of Francisco's jeans lay folded neatly on the dresser. I turned my back on them. "Hello?"

"Hey, Reba, this is your cousin."

I have about five thousand cousins, but I knew Kate's voice immediately.

"Aunt Kate!"

"Busy Sunday morning?" she asked.

I always read my Bible on the mountainside on

Sundays, but I never went to church. Mostly because there was no one to take me. Mama used to take Pio, Miguel, and me to Mass when I was little, but not any more. "Why?" I asked Aunt Kate.

"Want to come with me to church? Our priest is on vacation, and the priest who's subbing is an animal trainer, too. Mostly dogs. But he sounds great."

Church was kind of a foreign place to me. When I went there, everyone else knew the songs and knew what to do, and I felt stupid. I was about to tell Kate no when I remembered that God had helped me a few months ago with a problem. There was this animal, a wolverine, that a bounty hunter was trying to kill. I asked God to help me save the wolverine. And he did. So maybe God wanted me to come to *his* place for a change, instead of always meeting with me up here in the mountains. I twisted the phone cord. "Will you pick me up?"

"Yeah," she said. "At nine-thirty, okay?"

"Okay," I said. Then, panic-stricken, I asked, "Do I gotta wear a dress?"

Kate laughed. "You little burrito." She rolled her r's nicely, too. "You wear what you want."

We hung up and I skipped out of the bedroom. "What did Kate want?" asked Mama. She'd finished with the tortillas and sat at the kitchen table with her account books spread out.

"To take me to church on Sunday."

"That girl. She's wild one minute and so pi the next."

"Pi?"

Mama smiled. "Pious. I went to Catholic schools

all my life, remember? Anyone who acted holier-than-thou we called pi's."

"I don't think Kate is holier-than-thou," I said slowly.

Mama just grunted and bent over her books. I crept toward the tortillas.

"No more!" she snapped. "Dinner in an hour."

Honestly. She could see me with her eyes closed. I went back out, got the big flashlight down from the tack room, and called Burrito. We'd visit the cave again before dinner, and I would get a better look inside.

4
Into
the
Dark

We climbed the steep trail toward Mt. Wilson, Burrito and I. A small side trail, an animal trail, meandered along the side of the mountain. That trail led to the cave entrance. How had we missed it all this time? I'd walked past it a million times, at least.

Burrito ambled after me, examining patches of weeds, munching the most awful-looking dry ones. I waited for him at a big oak, and when he caught up he pressed his muzzle under my arm in a burro hug.

How could I leave him?

"I just won't, Burrito," I said. "We'll live up here." There were plenty of patches of grass and weeds around for him to graze. Now I had a place to live. The cave.

An added bonus: I wouldn't have to do that ten-page term paper after all. I'd run away before it was due. Cheered up considerably, I hurried on to the line of eucalyptus trees, their slender branches trembling in the high breeze, their many leaves flapping like feathers in birds' wings. Burrito scratched his side on a tree trunk, groaning with pleasure.

"Geez, like I never brush you," I told him.

The trail was narrow, barely wide enough for a burro and a person to walk side by side. Where was that cave? The line of eucalyptus trees was about an eighth of a mile long. I should have marked the spot or something—although I didn't want anyone else to find it.

The entrance had to be in the bushes somewhere. I parted some familiar-looking manzanita bushes. But behind the branches and the dark, shiny green leaves, only the dirt flank of the mountainside.

Funny. I had thought it was right here, by the big, bent-over oak tree. I knelt on the ground, hoping to feel the cool breeze from the cave's mouth. But no coolness touched my face.

I grabbed a long stick and poked around in other bushes. Nothing but more bushes and dirt.

Burrito finished scratching both sides and began grazing some fine young rye shoots, switching his bottlebrush tail.

If Sean were here, he'd remember where the cave was. He was good at details.

How had we missed finding that cave all this time? Maybe during an earthquake—there had been several just in the last two years—dirt had moved off the cave entrance. And then maybe the recent rains washed more dirt away from the opening.

Good theory anyway. I poked through more bushes and got scratched across the chin for my trouble.

Now wait, I thought. *My footprints from yesterday should show me the cave entrance.* But now my footprints were everywhere. Rats. I blew that.

But maybe a footprint close to bushes I hadn't yet checked?

Anytime I saw one of my footprints near the bushes, I parted the tangle of manzanita. Still nothing.

Could I be at the wrong place? Uncle Hector told stories of men getting lost in the mountains, circling, never getting home. I studied the waving line of trees. No way. This was it.

But I'd looked through all the bushes. How could I have missed it? Had there been an earthquake last night that buried it? Not hardly, unless it was an earthquake in one tiny place. Could there have been a cave-in because I'd been poking around? Could God be telling me I shouldn't run away? I didn't like that thought. Surely God understood that I *had* to stay here, that I was practically being forced to run away.

Burrito, a piece of grass hanging out of his mouth, stood smiling, his upper lip curled up, his eyes half closed, his nostrils flared wide pulling in mountain scents. A breeze ran through his stubby mane.

I licked my finger and held it up. No wind near me.

"Burrito, you caver, you," I said and put my hand on his neck. The cave breathed moistness over my arm. "You found the cave," I said and kissed his soft nose like Aunt Kate does.

Following the slow, hesitant breeze, I parted the manzanita and mountain mahogany bushes and pushed my way through. A branch scratched my arm; blood oozed up. The breeze, cool and damp, slid comfortingly over my face. I shifted more bushes and the mouth of the cave opened up, dark and yawning. I snapped on the flashlight, and the interior sprang up like an exposed ghost.

I looked back once at Burrito. He watched quietly, curiously, his long, fuzzy ears upright, his gaze softer than any pillow—then I ducked my head under the rocky overhang and stepped into the dark.

The flashlight beam bounced off rough, rocky walls. Beads of moisture seeped down rocky sides like trickles of sweat. Gold flecks glittered in the rock walls. I stepped closer and shone the light right on the veined rocks. Softly I touched the flakes. No, not gold, but mica. Bits of perfect glitter, bigger than any you could buy in a store, gleamed together like a starry night.

I moved slowly down the tunnel. The walls stretched up so high that I didn't have to duck my head. Yet the tunnel was narrow enough that when I held out my arms, my hands touched both rocky sides.

About twenty feet down, a long bolt of thick rock hung from the ceiling, like a dark icicle. Carefully I stepped around it, stopped, and lightly touched it. Stone crumbled under my fingers, like toast crumbs. Weird.

On I walked. The cave darkness was a deeper

black than moonless mountains. And I knew about the mountains at night; I'd spent more than one night in the San Gabriels, but on their surface. Now I was inside. Goose bumps rose on my arms.

Could I really live in here? I remembered reading in my Bible that King David had lived in caves when Saul was chasing him, trying to kill him. If King David could live in a cave, then so could I.

My light beam bounced off the walls. At home in the night stable, the flashlight was cheerfully bold. But here, the light was thin as an old man's arm. The cave darkness seemed to gobble up the light, chasing it back into the flashlight. I flashed it upward; it soared into darkness, like deep space must appear, seemingly endless. How high was the cave ceiling?

Something moved overhead. I pressed against the hard tunnel side, slightly panicked. A flutter of wings, faint squeaking. Birds—no. Bats. They lived in caves. Instantly I crouched. More wings shuffled, the squeaky voices dropping down like stones in water.

Get a grip, Reba, I told myself. *The light must bother them. Bats are harmless. They eat insects.*

Unless they're vampire bats!

Carefully I kept the beam down low, away from the ceiling, and the rustling died down. My flesh crawled as I thought of bats and fangs and blood. But then, vampire bats weren't indigenous (Sean's word kept haunting me) to the San Gabriels or even to North America. But that didn't mean vampire bats weren't here.

I walked on, the stone floor dipping away beneath my feet like the deck on a drunken ship. I hesitated, the soles of my feet tingling. Should I go on? I had already walked probably a quarter of a mile in. Should I go back and wait for Sean's help tomorrow?

I lifted the beam. The cave took a turn ahead. Maybe I'd just look around that bend, then go out.

I took a step, and the ground dropped out from under me.

5

The Inside of the Mountain

No time to scream.

I tumbled through cool darkness. My flailing hand hit rock and scraped off skin. Then came the jolt. The hard hitting of ground. I landed on my rear end like the time Uncle Hector's Medicine Hat horse threw me.

My flashlight beam rippled over rocks, rolling, then halted, flickering, when the flashlight banged against rock.

Oh God, no, don't let it be broken! Then it flared on, holding back the ever-present dark. I tensed, afraid to move, afraid to even reach for the flashlight in fear I'd fall again.

Into my thoughts sprang a horrible story I'd once read in a newspaper: A man who had been caving had fallen down a pit, like me. Only he landed on a soft something. When he flicked on his light it was the decaying carcass of a horse. Gross. At least I wasn't sitting in a dead horse's body.

Slowly I touched the ground in a circle around me. Stone, more stone, thank God. Some dirt on the surface of the rock. Before me was a line of dirt, then emptiness.

I swallowed and drew back my hand. I must be on a ledge. I had to see how big, or how small, the ledge was.

Slowly I reached for the light, stretching my arm long. My fingers closed on the dented handle. *Gotcha.* I shined the beam around me. Like I thought, in front of me was gaping blackness—if I'd fallen only inches ahead, I might still be falling, to who knows where. Maybe the center of the earth. To my left was a solid wall and to my right the ledge lowered itself like a burro dropping its neck to graze. A graceful slant down to who knew what.

With shaky knees, I stood, pressed against the rocky wall. The tunnel above looked about a foot taller than me, so actually I only—only!—fell about six feet.

Rocks jutted out of the wall here and there. I just might be able to climb back up.

It was then I realized how incredibly stupid I'd been to come here alone. No one knew where I was. Only Sean had an idea, but he didn't know exactly where the cave was.

My heart hammered. I was sweating in places I didn't know could sweat.

Help, God. Please.

I tried to relax. I took a couple of deep breaths like Mama says to do before you have to take a big test. My heartbeat slowed. I definitely wasn't going to climb down, no matter how gentle the path looked on the right. Not yet. I'd wait for Sean, and even then, we'd have to make some careful plans.

Stupid me. What was I thinking? Just like they say, you shouldn't climb mountains alone—although I did, thousands of times. But at least Mama and Maury (our local ranger) knew where I was most of the time and it wasn't like I was climbing Mt. Baldy in hundred-mile-an-hour winds or something. Caving was like climbing a mountain, except you're inside the mountain.

Standing on my tiptoes I carefully examined the wall. I tugged at jutting rocks to be sure they'd be firm handholds and footholds. One was loose. I'd avoid that one. I tucked the flashlight into my waistband. I'd need both hands.

At home my brothers and I used to play around and literally climb the walls on rainy days. We'd go into a corner and, with a foot and a hand planted firmly on one wall, the other foot on the other wall, we'd walk up the wall.

Only a couple of steps, then I'd be able to reach the lip of the ledge above me where I'd fallen. *Please, God, let it be firm.* I didn't want to think what might happen if I began to pull myself up only to have the ledge crumble.

I slowly began to climb. My legs ached and my

fingers tore at the rocks. A step. Another step. Then reaching for the ledge. With trembling arm muscles, I gripped the edge and pulled myself up. The flashlight dug into my stomach.

But the ledge held—*thank you, thank you, God*—and I hauled myself out of the pit and crawled onto the floor of the tunnel. I snatched the flashlight from my waistband, illuminating the ground—who knew if there might be another pit nearby—and moved away from the edge.

When I was safe, my knees gave way and I collapsed onto the ground. No wonder people kissed the ground when they were rescued.

I moved my feet and sat up; the pebbles I dislodged rattled down the pit, bouncing against the sides, ending in a quiet splash.

Water.

I must be imagining things.

Later I wondered if I had passed out for a few minutes. I sort of came to staring at the beam of the flashlight, listening to my teeth chatter with cold. I hadn't worn a sweater because it was so hot outside. But in here it was about forty degrees. Time to get out.

My legs, though aching, worked and I hiked back out, practically running toward the opening. Bats fluttered above me, but I just raced past them.

I burst through the bushes and into the daylight. Burrito started and pointed his ears at me. The sunlight was brilliant; I had to shade my eyes. Burrito rushed over, nuzzling me, as if to say, "Where have you been? I was so worried."

I was worried, too. I put my arms around his solid warmth and clung to him.

This time, I gathered three stones and stacked them across the trail from the entrance. Now that I was safe and standing in the light, I very much wanted to visit the cave again—but visit it safely.

Not now. I'd wait for Sean. Burrito and I walked back along the trail. As we crossed the ridge and dropped down into the canyon, the flashlight made a funny rattling sound. I'd forgotten to turn it off. I lifted it, clicked it off, and saw that the plastic cover over the bulb was splintered. A little piece of plastic rattled against the bulb. Geez, if it had gone out—

I shuddered, imagining being on that ledge without light. And no one, *no one* would know where I was. That gave new fodder to my nightmares. Burrito pressed against my side and looked up with dark eyes.

6
No Burros in the City

Back home, Francisco's truck was parked next to our house. But I was too tired and too busy thinking to react. The burros were already in the stable munching dinner. With aching arms, I brushed Burrito in his stall while he thrust his head into the wooden manger and ate noisily. Then I slid down into the shavings beside my baby burro. I would just rest for a moment.

"Reba?" The voice came from a long way away. I woke instantly. The barn was flooded with light.

Francisco's heavy footsteps clumped down the aisle. Burrito stood, one hind leg cocked, his ear forward.

"Are you in here?" asked Francisco.

I struggled up, shavings clinging to my jeans, then falling off like flakes of snow. "Yeah," I said, rough with sleep. At least my knees held me up and my arms had stopped aching.

"Your mama thought she saw you come in here a while ago," he said and hung his arms over the top of Burrito's stall door. Mama saw all. When I was little, I used to think she could read my mind. Even now I sometimes wondered.

Francisco backed up as I opened the stall door. "Did you fall asleep in there?" he asked me.

Did you figure that out all by yourself? I thought nastily.

Halfway down the aisle, Francisco caught my arm. "I want us to be friends, Reba," he said again, like he had in the car the other night. The man never gave up.

"Please, Reba."

Impossible, I snapped back in my thoughts.

Francisco put his foot on a bale of straw we left there only for show—like an advertisement, like, *Look, this is a stable. Come rent a burro.* It had been sitting there for years; rats had raided it for nesting material.

"Talk to me, Reba," he said, his brow wrinkling. "Let me know what you're thinking."

You don't want to know, I thought.

Francisco tugged on pant legs and began to sit on the bale.

"That bale is probably hollow," I said. "It might—"

It did.

It broke in half. Francisco tumbled ungracefully into the aisle, startling the nearby burro. If anyone else had fallen through that bale, it might have been funny, but my first thought was that if Francisco told Mama, she might think I had planned this. Had I? Subconsciously? No. Francisco had come to me to talk, not the other way around.

Should I reach out and help him up? But just as suddenly as he'd gone down, Francisco came up grinning, arms flung out as if he'd just completed some trick.

"Are you okay?" I asked him.

He straightened and put his hand on his heart. "So you do care, Reba!"

I had to smile. He looked so silly.

"Can't we be friends?" he asked again.

His ruddy brown face beamed at me, like a cheerful dog. He had straw hanging from his corduroy pants. Okay, I guess I could be glad for Mama that she had another grown-up to help her out. But why did she have to marry him? Why couldn't they just sort of hang out together?

"Friends have to be friends on both sides," I said slowly. Then I stopped, horrified at my words.

"I see," he said after a pause. All his beaming went out, like a flashlight snapped off. "I'm sorry you feel that way, Reba."

I'm not sorry, I thought fiercely, my anger shifting into gear. "My whole life is changing because of you and they aren't good changes either. I don't want to leave. And I won't! You can't make me." I ran out of the barn and up to my Bible-reading ridge, stumbling over rocks in the dusk.

The wind trickled over me as I sat on an outcropping of granite. Part of me was saying, *Reba, it isn't Francisco's fault that your parents aren't together.*

No, but he hasn't helped things.

The front-door screen slammed below me. Mama would be livid when he told her what I'd said to him.

And if my words weren't bad enough, it was the way I'd said them, the way I'd wielded them, like a fighting burro's hooves. Sharp, wanting to wound.

It was time to run away. I scooped up a handful of dirt and let it trickle through my fingers. Francisco and Mama would be happier without me, and I'd be happier without them.

I sat up there and figured out what stuff I'd need, thinking of ways to carry supplies out to the cave. No school for me anymore, but maybe eventually I could go to the library and read. I did like to learn things that I wanted to learn. Maybe later I could even build myself a cabin like Uncle Hector had built his. Anyway, I'd live in the mountains forever. When I finally went back down home, I was satisfied that I could manage on my own in the mountains. So when Mama sent me to my room for being rude to Francisco, I didn't mind so much. I just lay on my bed and thought about my new life.

Saturday morning after breakfast, Mama gave out commands. Francisco had left already. Last night I had skipped dinner so I wouldn't have to see Francisco again.

"Miguel and Andres work the store this morning," said Mama. They both groaned. Our little country store sold cold drinks, candy, and ice cream to hikers and picnickers.

"Mama," complained Miguel, "I did it last Saturday. It's Reba's turn."

"So you'll do it again," she said, then added, "Only a few more weeks, now."

My fingers froze over the dishes I was rinsing, even though I knew I wouldn't be going with them. But so soon. So soon they would be gone.

Andres asked, "When are we moving?"

"Spring break," said Mama, glancing at me a little nervously. Spring break was a little over two weeks away.

"We found a place to rent," said Mama.

"How many bedrooms?" asked Miguel.

"Three," said Mama. "You and Andres will have to share."

Miguel complained loudly.

"What about Pio?" I asked.

"He's staying in Pasadena to keep going to school," she said. "It's too far to commute. So he's looking for an apartment with a couple of other college students."

"So can I have Burrito then, since Pio wouldn't be living with us?" I said. I had to argue or Mama would suspect I was up to something.

Andres gave a hoot. "A burro in the city!"

"Why not?" I demanded. "If Pio isn't around eating tons of food. Besides, Burrito doesn't eat much. He could eat the lawn so no one has to mow it."

"You can't have a burro in the city," said Miguel. He reached over and turned off the faucet.

"Why not?" I asked again.

"Because," said Miguel in disgust. "You just can't."

Mama carried the last of the breakfast dishes over to the sink for me to wash. "No burros in the city," she said quietly. "I'm sorry."

Sure you are, I thought rudely, filling up the sink with hot water and soap suds.

Miguel and Andres filed out to open the store. Mama called, "Reba, I'll need your help today packing some things."

I jabbed at the soap suds. "I had plans with Sean."

"I need you, Reba," she said. "This is going to be a busy time for us all."

I told myself grimly that I'd have lots of time to explore the cave once I moved in there. Waiting a few more days wouldn't make that much difference.

7

The
Stuff of
Nightmares

On Sunday morning, I woke early, let the burros out into the pasture, and fed them out there. Then I waited outside, sitting on the porch, watching the burros in the sunlight. Definitely I'd take Burrito with me. He was broken to hobble, a piece of leather tying his front legs together about six inches apart. A hobble kept a horse or burro from traveling far. So I could live in the cave and hobble him in different places to graze.

No, I wouldn't leave him behind.

Aunt Kate drove up and we rumbled off to her church.

The priest there talked mostly about dogs and the funny things they do, instead of about God, but it was okay. The people in the congregation listened hard. He explained how domestic animals have their own code of morality, which includes fitting in with humans and helping humans. Burrito was exactly that way.

After the service I wished I could talk to the priest-trainer, but he was mobbed by others. Anyway, I didn't really know what I'd say to him except, *I've got a burro who's just like the dogs you described. Only my mother wants to get rid of him.*

"Look," I said to Aunt Kate as we sat on the hard wooden pews, waiting for the big church to empty a little before we made our way down the aisle. The colors from a stained-glass window poured over us, blue and purple with crimson on the edges. I touched the colors and they slid over my fingers.

Kate smiled and scooped the colors into her palm. She was one of the most beautiful girls around. Nothing like the blonde fluff you see in movies. She was tall and strong. She had black hair to her waist and big brown eyes and a dazzling smile. Sean teases me and says I have a crush on her. I don't. I just like her a lot.

The stained-glass colors danced over the diamond ring on her left hand that marked her start on a journey where I couldn't follow. At least not for a long time.

As we walked across the blacktop parking lot, she waved at several people. One guy, probably thirty or so, ran up to her. A priest, I think. He had white robes on and a big cross around his neck.

"I'll miss class on Friday," said the priest, or whatever he was. "I'm going to that retreat after all."

"No problem," said Kate. "I'll call you tonight and tell you what's on the exam. That's the main thing." She patted him reassuringly on the shoulder like he was her pet. He trotted off, calling to people and waving.

Kate unlocked the passenger side door of her old Toyota. I slid in and unlocked the door on her side. When she started the engine, I asked, "Who was the guy?"

"Father Delgato? He's one of my students."

I laughed to think of a priest being one of her students.

She grinned, knowing why I laughed. "He's smart," she said. "He wants to get his degree in physics." Kate taught undergraduates at CalTech, where she was getting her Ph.D. Last year she'd finished her Master's at MIT and moved back here.

"Mama says you were wild when you were younger," I told her, then regretted it when Kate's face hardened. But wild wasn't always bad, was it?

"She does, does she?" said Kate. She put the little Toyota in gear and drove us out of the church parking lot. Her long fingers tapped the padded steering wheel. "Well, I guess she's seen me at my worst."

I tried to remember Kate at her worst. "I guess Mama kept me away from you when you were at your worst," I said, "because I don't remember you ever being bad."

"Well, it was light years ago. When I was thirteen, fourteen. You weren't very old."

"I was three or four."

"That's not very old."

Old enough that I remembered clearly the day Papa walked out on us.

Miguel and Pio were in grade school. Andres was only a tiny baby. I remember him in his crib, crying at the top of his lungs. I was clinging to my stuffed monkey on the floor, terrified. The only thing louder than baby Andres's cries was Mama screaming at Papa.

Her words were like tumbling grey floodwater rushing at me. *Just get out then!*

So Papa got out. He never took anything with him. He left clothes, books, music cassettes, everything. But he took our family away from us, just the same.

When Papa slammed the door, I got up and stood at the window, listening to Papa's engine roar loud, then get softer as it disappeared. My feelings for Papa were like that—strong at first, but as time went by they grew distorted and faint.

This part I don't remember, but Mama said I became fearful for months. I was afraid to be alone. I had clung to her and to my brothers. I had refused to sleep alone for a whole year. Andres and I shared a room—even a baby was someone—until Mama finally said we needed our own rooms.

I don't remember the fear, but I do have this nightmare. Most kids have nightmares about being chased by monsters. Even Sean has nightmares about this werecoyote going after him. But my nightmare is being in the dark, alone, like in outer space where time is frozen. Nothing moves. No one answers me, no matter how loud I call out.

I told Sean about that nightmare and he told his mother, who's a psychologist, and she said I have that dream because I feel abandoned. Papa only writes at Christmastime and on our birthdays, and even that sounds forced, like he's a long-forgotten relative. So if I feel abandoned it's not surprising. But I still have that nightmare. And every time I have it, I get scared silly and I crawl into bed with Andres and listen to him breathe until I can fall asleep.

Kate made her little car fly along the freeway, passing up bigger cars and trucks. I like going fast. I rolled the window down a crack and let the wind pour over my head, like baptizing waters.

"Do you have nightmares?" I asked her.

"Oh, yes," she said and flung back her hair.

"What about?" I asked.

"That this great grey wolf is after me."

"Does he catch you?"

"He hasn't yet."

I sighed, knowingly.

She squeezed my arm and we smiled at each other. Maybe when I run away, I could sometimes stay with Kate. I don't think she would tell on me. But then she's getting married this summer, so maybe not. I sighed again and let the wind continue to pour over me.

8

They're Gone

At home Francisco's truck was still parked in the lot. When we drove up, Mama came outside and leaned in Kate's car window. "Stay for lunch?" she asked Kate.

Kate shrugged at me and I nodded. "Okay, Aunt Kela," she said. Mama called the boys to lunch and went back in, the screen door banging.

I raised my eyebrows at Kate and she said, "Don't look a gift horse in the mouth."

"Or a gift burro's mouth."

We giggled and went inside. But I knew what Kate

meant. Something was up. I moved inside behind Kate like a wary burro.

Mama had fixed a big taco lunch, with olives, jalapeños, diced tomatoes from our garden, lettuce, all the fixings. My brothers, including Pio with Jessica, were in the kitchen.

"Help yourselves," said Francisco expansively and waved his arms. I picked up a plate. Kate chatted with Jessica. Andres bumped my ribs with his elbow.

"Hey," I said.

He gave me a solemn look. "Bad news," he said.

I whirled and faced him. "What?"

"A truck came this morning after you went with Aunt Kate," he whispered. My fingers dug into my palms.

"A truck? What about it?"

"The burros," he said. "They're gone. Sold." I looked out the kitchen window at the burros' pasture. Empty.

While I was at church they'd been taken. Mama had wanted me out of the house. I dropped my plate on the floor with a crash and ran for the barn, just in case Andres was somehow wrong.

Mama called my name. I ignored her and leaped off the porch and ran down the dirt path to the barn. No burros. I flung myself back outside and ran to the gate to the pasture. No burros. Only their hoofprints and their D & D to show they had once been here.

I would have screamed if I'd thought I could split the mountains and bury us all. But instead shoved my fist into my mouth.

No. No. No.

An arm touched me. I whirled around.

Kate.

"Reba," she said, her eyes huge. "I'm so sorry."

"Did you know?" I demanded. If she had been in with Mama I'd, I'd—I don't know what I'd do but it would be bad.

"No. Never behind your back, Reba." She put both arms around me and I let her hold me. We stood for a long time, the wind trickling over us. I didn't dare look up at the empty pasture.

That was it. I was leaving. Tonight.

"Where is he?" I asked Mama later, after Francisco and Andres had taken a truckful of packed boxes to Santa Ana. Miguel was watching the store; Pio and Jessica had left. Kate had lingered, washing dishes, tidying up in the kitchen while Mama continued to pack boxes. My whole world had tilted. But I didn't care anymore. I had been plotting in my room, putting my belongings in my backpack.

Mama didn't answer. She was wrapping serving bowls and special dishes in newspaper. Kate was helping her quietly. I figured after I was gone for a few weeks, and they'd moved to Santa Ana, I could work on getting Burrito back from the Sierra pack station. But which one was it?

"Where is Burrito?" I asked her.

Finally she sat back. "He's on his way to the Sierra, to another pack station."

"I know that. What's the name of it?" I stood on one foot, then the other. She didn't answer. It didn't matter. I could call every pack station until I found him. I'd somehow rent a trailer and get him back. I would. I would. I would.

"Tell me," I insisted.

Mama's mouth tightened. "You don't need to know it," she said. "He's sold and that's it, Reba."

"You could have at least told me. You could have at least—"

"Stop it!" Mama straightened, her black gaze searing me. "They needed to be sold." I glared back.

She continued in a hard voice, like unplowed ground, "You have done just about everything possible to create problems. I'm sick of it. Your behavior is incredibly selfish. We are moving to Santa Ana. Francisco will be your stepfather. Like it or not. Now get out of my sight!"

I fled to my room, fuming. I would be out of her sight permanently. I shut my door and finished packing. One of those lightweight space blankets we used when we camped. A change of clothes. I'd wear as much as possible tonight. A notepad to draw on. Food I'd get tonight, and a pot to cook in. After a minute, I picked up my Bible and stuffed it in, too.

A couple of hours later Kate knocked on my door. "What?" I asked ungraciously and hid my pack under the bed. She came in and sat on my bed.

"Reba, really I'm sorry about—about this all. About Burrito."

"Me, too," I muttered.

"I asked Aunt Kela if you could come stay with me until you moved. Would that help? At least you'd get a break from everyone. You'd have to sleep on the floor of my room, but if you don't mind, I don't mind."

Tears threatened, but I choked them back. If I hadn't been planning to run away, I'd have gone with her. "I don't think so," I said. "But thanks."

She got up. "I've gotta get back home now. I'll talk to you soon, okay?"

I nodded. She wouldn't be able to. No one would.

She drove off. Everyone else left me alone. I lay on my bed and dozed. Usually when I take naps during the day, I don't dream, but I did then. I dreamed I was in the cave, only it was a magic cave with rooms filled with food and toys. Everything glittered and glistened in a magical light.

In my dream, one day I left the cave and ran up the canyon to the pack station. But it was empty, emptier than it had been this afternoon. The gate creaked on its hinges.

"They're gone," said a familiar voice.

I turned. It was the animal I had helped last November, the wolverine I helped save from the bounty hunter.

The wolverine sat in an easy chair in the shade, picking his teeth with a long front nail. "They're all gone," he repeated.

"But where?" I asked.

"Everyone has grown up and gone away."

"Even Sean?"

"He's married and has two kids of his own."

No!

The wolverine gave a snarly laugh, his bushy tail flicking in the air, and walked away.

They had all left me.

No. Not really. I'd left them.

9
The
Great
Plan

When I woke it was dark outside and only a nightlight burned in the bathroom. I groped through the hallway to the living room and turned on a lamp. A note was on the coffee table.

Reba,
   We went out to eat and to a movie. Took Miguel and Andres with us. Be back by ten.

                    Mama and Francisco

It was seven now. My head unfogged quickly— this had to be the night. While Mama and the others were at dinner, I could pack all my stuff and food out to the cave before they got back. Perfect.

Except Burrito was gone.

At least he was with his family; I hoped the Sierra pack station would keep him near Mojo, his sire, and the others. *Please God, take care of him.* God feeds the sparrow, so he would care for a baby burro, wouldn't he?

I made two trips to the cave with my backpack, carrying clothes and food. The night was clear, cold, and dark, with a scattering of silver stuff. At nine-thirty, I finished my second trip and packed my pack with the last load. I stood looking around the house. I touched the back of the couch, the coffee table where Mama did her account books, then went into the kitchen. I picked up the phone and dialed Sean's number.

"Hello?" his mom answered.

"May I speak to Sean?"

"It's rather late. Is this Reba?"

"Yeah." I held my breath. Please let me talk to Sean. "It's important," I said.

She gave a noisy sigh and I heard her call, "Sean, phone. It's that Reba."

That Reba.

Sean came on and said, "Reba?" in a surprised voice. I could have cried right then, but I didn't.

"I'm going, Sean," I said. "I wanted to tell you because—" Because you're the only one who cares.

"To the cave?" he asked.

"Is your mom there?" If she heard him—

"Nah, she's watching TV. Give me a couple hours, and after they go to bed I'll meet you."

"You can't."

"Yes I can. You shouldn't go alone. What if you fall again, only worse?"

I had thought of that. It was a scary thought.

"I'll meet you at the trailhead, okay?" His voice was low, so I almost didn't hear him.

"What time?" I asked, thinking it might actually work out better this way. If I was still here when everybody came home at ten and then waited until they were all asleep before I took off, I'd have the whole night before they knew I was gone. But if I was gone when Mama got back at ten, she'd notice and start looking right away. Or maybe she wouldn't. Maybe she would be glad I was gone. I should leave a note telling them not to look for me. Tears of self-pity burned my eyes.

Sean said, "How about 1:30? That'll give me time to get up there."

It took about forty-five minutes by bike to come up the road, or about a half hour to walk up the mountain on the little trail. I swallowed my tears and told him, "Be careful. Bring a flashlight and batteries, okay?"

"Okay. Are you bringing Burrito?"

My throat tightened. "No."

"Well, you can get him later."

Another sob threatened. I'd tell him later. "You be careful, Sean," was all I said, and we hung up.

It was getting close to ten o'clock, so I hid my pack under the bed, got into my nightgown, and tried to relax. I listened to the radio, letting the music curl over me like waves. When Francisco's truck rumbled outside, I leaped up, turned off my light, and pretended to be asleep.

The front door opened and closed quietly. The murmur of Mama's voice mixed with the boys' voices, and Francisco's.

"Go brush your teeth, Andres. Hurry up. Miguel, you too. School tomorrow, you know."

But not for me.

The pipes rattled in the bathroom. Andres was chattering about the movie they'd seen and Miguel was saying, "You're nuts, Andres. That was the bad guy." My bedroom door creaked and Mama slipped in.

"Reba?"

I made a murmuring sound like I was deep asleep and turned over. Francisco whispered from the doorway, "She asleep?"

"Yes." Mama smoothed my forehead. I tried to breath slowly and deep.

"Hard day for her," said Francisco.

"She was her father's favorite," said Mama. "She's always taken this so hard."

"I still think we should have let her keep the little burro," said Francisco.

I held my breath. Francisco saying that?

Mama drew the blanket up over my shoulder. "No. A clean break is best."

I wanted to sit up and shriek, *If you had let me keep Burrito, I wouldn't have to run away!*

But of course I couldn't. Not now. I had packed out my gear; Sean was coming; it was too late to stop now.

10
The
Night

I had set my alarm for 1:15 and stretched the cord to put the clock under my pillow, but it turned out that I didn't need it. I woke automatically at 1:14, turned off the alarm, and sat up.

Now. Time to go.

Without turning on the light I pulled off my nightgown and, shivering, pulled on tights, long underwear, jeans, t-shirt, flannel shirt, pullover sweater, and my jacket. Then two pairs of socks and my tennis shoes. I shouldered my pack.

The clock read 1:24.

Should I write a note?

An image of Mama flowed into my thoughts. By the beginning of third grade I could barely read. I would hunch down, terrified that the teacher would call on me to read out loud and I wouldn't be able to say the slippery words that shone on the pages of our books.

But the teacher did call on me. And I did fall over the treacherous words. Then wept. Not in class, never in front of the kids or teachers. But at home in the barn. Mama found me.

"*Mi hija*, what?" she had asked.

I could only hold out the awful book with the words that fled from me.

So patiently, every day after school, we sat out on the porch and went through enemy words until they became friends. Mama found some books on burros, on the mountains—grown-up books, not dumb kid stuff, like "See Jane run." After we looked at the pictures, she would teach me the sounds of the letters, the taste of the words, what to look for, what words were tricky and sly and ways to snare them and make them my captives and then my friends.

I searched for a piece of paper and a pen. I wrote in the light of the face of the clock:

Mama,
    I can't move to Santa Ana.
    I love the mountains too much.
    I'm fine and with a friend.

I didn't want to betray Sean in case he had written something else to his parents, maybe that he had run away to be in a circus or who knew what—although Mama would probably figure out who "a friend" was anyway.

Then I signed it:

Love, Rebecca

She'd understand what I meant with my full name.

I crept through the sleeping house. I'd especially miss Andres, my baby brother who wasn't a baby anymore. He'd be grown up when I saw him again. I blinked back more tears.

Quietly I unlocked the front door, slipped out, locked it behind me, then leaped from the porch, the backpack slamming down on my spine.

I was free!

A couple of cars were parked in the upper lot. Hikers on overnights. The mountains could be brutal at night. Once when the winds were up to a hundred miles an hour on Mt. Baldy, the search-and-rescue people had to hunt for a lost woman and boy. The rescue people had to crawl on the trails, or else they'd have been blown off the mountain. I was glad we'd be safe in the cave.

The sky was like a blank blackboard, no stars, no moon. Distant city lights reflected in the cloud cover, and the whole night sort of glowed with a pale light.

I walked the long way down past the ranger station and silently said goodbye to Maury sleeping in the back room. Then down to the lower parking lot and to the trailhead.

No Sean yet. I hadn't brought a watch, so I settled

down to wait, sitting on the cold ground in a deeper shadow, just in case someone should appear, like hikers returning at weird hours.

I waited in the deep silence, not really feeling the cold through my thick clothes, but shivering anyway.

Then I heard steps. Someone breathing. Sean's bright hair bobbed down the road. I jumped up and could have thrown my arms around him. I didn't, of course.

He stopped in front of me, a daypack on his back.

"Hi," I said.

"Hi." And we grinned huge grins at each other.

"So this is it, huh?" he said.

I nodded, awed at our choice.

"Show me this cave," he said, breaking the moment, and we began down the trailhead.

The canyon was thickly black, but that didn't matter; we could practically walk the trails blindfolded.

"I wish I had a dollar for every time I've walked this canyon," said Sean after we'd gone several turns down the path, away from Chantry Flat, away from anyone who would hear us. I wished I'd thought to bring mittens. I stuffed my hands into my jacket pockets.

"What would you do with the dollars?" I asked.

"Buy a really good motor scooter so I wouldn't have to walk all over the place."

"But you're not old enough to have a license," I said.

He shrugged, the nylon of his jacket hissing. "I will be in a few years. The sky is kind of glowing, isn't it?"

The clouds pulsed softly. Like they held a gentle secret.

"How about you?" he asked.

"What?" I pulled my attention away from the clouds.

"What would you buy if you got lots of money?"

I would have said something else a few months ago, but now it was, "Buy back the pack station and pay for the whole thing so we wouldn't have to make payments on it anymore. And I'd make it better. Like with riding horses, so more people would come up here and we'd make more money." That had been Mama's dream before Francisco. But he had changed everything.

"How practical you are," said Sean.

"I have to be," I said.

"Well, maybe we'll find treasure in the cave," he said. "Indian gold and jewels."

We were quiet, thinking about heaps of gems and gold coins.

"You know," I said, "they did use to mine gold up here."

"And silver," said Sean. "Do you think you just found a mine shaft?"

"I hope not. I don't think so." A mine shaft would be awfully boring.

We hiked into the canyon, then took a side trail up the mountain's flank. We walked a long time, it seemed, before we smelled the sinus-clearing scent of eucalyptus trees drawing us forward.

Now if I could remember exactly where the entrance was. I hunted for the landslide, the rumpled ground.

"It's here?" asked Sean. "We've walked near here a billion times."

"I know."

Sean poked around in the bushes.

"I put three stones in a pile," I said, "across from the entrance. But now I can't find the stones."

Then Sean said with awe in his voice, "Something smells damp." His hair blew slightly, but there wasn't a wind tonight.

"You found the cave," I said, pleased.

11
The
Art
Gallery

While Sean parted the branches carefully, I snapped on my flashlight and shot the beam into the cave mouth. The pale light sparkled over the bits of mica embedded in the granite.

"The cave's breathing," murmured Sean, his hair moving gently in the cool, moist wind.

"I know," I said. The cave was alive.

Sean gave me an expectant look. "Ready?"

My heart began to hammer like it had after I'd fallen into the pit. I could see myself falling, hitting the ledge, then bouncing off, falling again into the black pit—

Stop! You're just scaring yourself, I told myself. *With Sean here that won't happen. Or at least, it won't happen so easily.*

No. It won't happen.

"Maybe we should rope ourselves together," I said. "Like mountain climbers do."

"Did you bring rope?" he asked.

I showed him my cache from earlier in the night. I had brought a couple coils of cotton rope.

Sean wrapped the rope around my waist, tying the knot at the small of my back. He left about twelve feet limp between us, then knotted the rope around him.

"Ready?" he asked.

I took a deep breath of the night air and answered, "Yeah."

We plunged into the cave.

The air was cooler inside and moister. I remembered hearing the sound of water when I was in the pit. Was that really what I'd heard? If so, I wanted to see the underground pool or whatever it was—but I didn't want to go down into the pit again.

"Wait," I said as we squeezed by the bolt of rock in the middle of the tunnel. "What is this called? Stalactite? Stalagmite? I can't keep them straight."

"Stalactite," said Sean in a hushed voice. "It's huge." He put both hands on it. The stalactite was nearly as big around as a full-grown burro and colored white and tan, almost the shade of Burrito's coat. Burrito. I wanted to howl for his loss. But no, the loss wouldn't be for long.

I stroked the stalactite and the toast-like crumbs

came off again. Maybe it was shedding like an animal does.

"So where's this pit?" asked Sean. "I don't want to fall into it."

"Ahead." I took the lead and played the beam over the stone floor so I'd see the pit.

The cave was silent except for our quiet steps. I stopped, uneasy. Why? What was missing? Oh, yeah, the rustling noise was gone. Of course. It was night. The bats would be outside. I tipped the flashlight up. Nothing moved outside.

"What's that smell?" asked Sean.

"Bat guano!" I laughed. It did stink!

Ahead was the turn in the tunnel. I slowed down. My light blazed along the floor.

And there was the crumbling hole, yawning. "Stop," I said and sat down. I wasn't taking any chances. I crawled up to the hole. Bits of dirt and rock moved under my fingers and tumbled over the edge. Sean panted over my shoulder. I shone the flashlight down. "You can see the ledge."

"Reba! It's so narrow."

It was. Only about two body widths. "I think God was taking care of me," I said. How else could I explain it?

Sean just gave a snort. "If he was taking care of you, you shouldn't have fallen in at all."

Was that true? Was it God's fault I was behaving stupidly? His responsibility to protect me from my dumbness? The murmur of water floated up. Sean caught his breath. "I've read about underground rivers," he said. So maybe it was more than just a pool.

"We definitely have to explore it," I said, "but I don't think I want to go down the pit now."

"Later," said Sean. "When we know more about the cave."

We. I was glad he was with me.

I flicked the beam out of the hole and across the pit.

The hole was only a couple of feet across, but it was nearly as wide as the tunnel floor, leaving only a small bit of stone footing on either side of the hole. I could jump over it—but what if the tunnel wasn't firm on the other side?

I lay quietly, thinking.

"Look," said Sean. His beam traced the edge of the hole, then explored the tight, narrow path next to the wall. "I bet we could walk right past this hole." Dust paraded in the light beam, glinting and gold. The hole looked like a dragon's mouth.

"You first," I said, ungraciously.

"Okay," he said and stood up.

"Wait a minute," I said and clambered up next to him. "If you fall in, how am I supposed to hold you? You weigh more than me."

He grinned. "You better go first, then."

"You tricked me!"

"You got a better way to cross this thing?"

I eyed the hole. "Okay," I said. "But if I fall, you sure better hold me up."

He just smiled in the dim light. "Of course I will. Do you think I want to fall, too?"

I stuck out my tongue at him. Then I glued myself to the cave wall. The lip around the hole was slick with water dripping—from where? Above? I'd better be careful or I'd slide in.

Carefully I took a step. The hole yawned, wide, hungry. I clutched the rough wall with my fingers and crept. A stone slid and Sean gasped when the stone hit water many seconds later.

"Careful," he said.

"I *am* being careful," I snapped.

Finally my feet touched the other side. I scrambled away from the hole and sat down. "Just you don't fall," I told him.

He delicately crossed. I aimed my flashlight before him, lighting his way better and holding my breath.

A puff of dust woofed over the hole and filtered down. Sean dropped to the ground beside me. "I'm safe, I'm safe." He kissed the ground.

"You're nuts," I said.

He straightened up. "Maybe we ought to keep ourselves tied together, just in case." I thought of our class unit on explorers of the South Pole, and how they fell into crevasses that were a huge network of caves under snow. "Good idea," I said.

We walked side by side along the passage, alert for any more pits. After another quarter mile or so, the tunnel opened up into a larger cavern.

Our beams flicked on the walls of the cave. Colored lines and dots and swirls covered the stone walls.

"What is this?" I asked.

"Not naturally occurring," said Sean. "Someone painted these."

I turned to the drawing closest to me. They weren't like graffiti you see on brick walls in the cities, or like taggers' names sprayed on the backs of freeway signs. No. These were light, airy lines of brown, rising and falling: mountains, people holding baskets, animals, the sun.

"It's an art gallery," I said suddenly.

12
A Quiet Memory

The rope around my waist gave a yank. "Hey," I protested.

"Sorry," said Sean. He was examining a drawing, his flashlight flickering. "These have got to be really old."

"My ancestors did them, I bet," I said.

He shot me a look, but said, "I wonder why they would come in the cave?"

Maybe they had things to run away from. I touched the old paint. It was smooth on the face of the rock. Brown lines rose in a mountain range with one peak bigger than them all, capped with white. "Mt. Baldy," I said.

"Yeah, and look, here's a huge bird," said Sean. "Pterodactyl!"

"I don't think the Indians lived here that long ago. It's probably a condor."

We started giggling.

"See how wide the wings look? Only condors look like that."

Condors had lived across much of Southern California long ago, but now they were all but extinct. The last wild ones had been captured a few years ago and put into zoos; only recently two had been set free again to see if it could live in the wilds. Was that the way of the world? Things dying only to come alive on an old cave wall?

We moved on, admiring the mostly brown-colored drawings—the Indians must have lived during droughts too.

Sean stopped so suddenly that I nearly walked into him. His flashlight beam swept around the cave. "Look at this," he said. The beam swirled again. "This is like a round room."

I turned. Sure enough. Our lights caught the curved, smooth walls arching in a circle, about as big as a kid's bedroom.

"Maybe it was a special honor to paint here," said Sean.

I squinted at the simple line drawings. "Maybe bad kids were kept here. It was the detention room."

"No, really," insisted Sean. "This is a weird place. So round. Almost like someone carved this room." We looked at each other. My hand touched the smooth rock. Could that be? Someone chiseled this round room?

"I bet they did," muttered Sean.

"Amazing," was all I could say. It must have taken forever, hammering and scraping away.

We came to the last drawing and bright wonder fell over me. "Look," whispered Sean. "Isn't that a—" he broke off. I crowded him aside and studied the drawing.

A person was painted in brown. It was a better drawing than most. Not just a stick person, but a figure with hair, round arms and legs, a face, holding out something in his hand.

Next to him was an animal.

"Not a dog," whispered Sean.

No. The animal was stroked in black and it had bold, pale stripes along its sides that ended in its bushy tail.

"A wolverine," I breathed. "There were wolverines in these mountains."

We had thought our wolverine—the one we had saved from the bounty hunter—was a rare appearance. And nowadays it was. But maybe back then there had been lots of them. I touched the wolverine drawing and traced the outline with my finger.

"It must be in your blood," said Sean, thickly. "To care for animals like you do." He jabbed his finger at the person near the wolverine. "It looks like he's giving him food." Like I had given our wolverine food to help him. But in turn he'd helped me, too. Deep inside me he had helped me.

"That will be your Indian name," said Sean. "Wolverine Girl."

I laughed to think of a white boy naming me. But then, why not?

"And you shall be One Who Says Crazy Things," I told him, and we laughed.

Finally we walked out of the art gallery, choosing one of the several tunnels leading out. How long since anyone else had studied those drawings? A hundred years? A thousand years?

We squeezed down a tunnel, climbing over some big rocks strewn in the tunnel. I banged my shin and knew I'd have a good-sized bruise.

"It goes down this way," said Sean.

I followed him, hopping off a rock flattened like a thick pancake.

The air was cold; here, it didn't move like someone breathing, as it had up by the manhole and the big stalactite. I blew on my fingers and tucked my left hand into my jacket pocket. With my right hand, I trained the flashlight beam on Sean's blue-jacketed back. His hair was bright as mica in the light.

"Maybe this cave goes on forever," I said.

"Forever?" asked Sean with scorn. "The earth is finite, you know."

"But maybe this is a magic tunnel," I said.

"Like Burrito is a magic burro, right?" He laughed.

Burrito. Not only my fingers were cold, but all of me now.

"Reba?" he asked, when my silence grew as stony as the cave walls.

I told him in a rush. "Burrito's gone. Mama sold

him and the others." Tears crowded in my eyes, but I wouldn't cry in front of Sean.

Sean stopped in the middle of the tunnel and turned around. The rope between us drooped. I stared at Sean's tennis shoes, imagining Burrito's little neat hooves and the way he picked his nimble feet up and trotted like a quick wild thing.

"I'm going to call all the pack stations in the Sierras," I said, still staring at Sean's shoes and neon-green shoelaces, "until I find out where he is. Then I'll tell them I'm coming for him. Selling him was a mistake. Somehow I'll get the money." I had no idea where.

Sean took a step closer. "Reba, I'm really sorry."

I finally looked up at him.

He had tears in his eyes.

I thought he was going to put his arms around me. Part of me would have straight-armed him, but part of me would have let him. As it was, we stood with the thought of the little pale burro between us.

13
A Wild Gift

The tunnel ran down and down. The air grew stiller and a little colder, like walking through deep sea water. Even through my jacket, when I stopped walking, the cold touched me. The tunnel remained big enough to walk through except in a few places where we had to crawl on our hands and knees. We stayed tied together, just in case.

After we had walked about two hours—it must have been four in the morning, at least—Sean said,

"Let's rest." We found a dry, sandy spot to sit and eat some dried fruit and sip water from a canteen.

"What's that noise?" I asked. It was a rushing sound. I hadn't noticed it until we sat still. Sean snapped off his flashlight, as if that would help him hear better.

"I don't hear anything," he said. "You and your heightened senses."

It was like the sound of wind in the trees, far off. Could we be closer to the surface than I'd thought? But we'd been going down; the muscles in my calves told me that. Although I might have been turned around. We'd been careful to mark on rocks with a big red felt marker whenever we chose a fork so we would know how to get back out, but I didn't know how deep we were. Maybe a thousand feet? Maybe more?

I yawned and my ears popped. I could hear the rushing sound better. "You can't hear that?" I asked.

"Nope."

"You're getting senile," I said.

"You're imagining things," he said.

"I'm not."

"You are."

"Not."

"Are."

"Not."

We packed our backpacks and argued on down the tunnel.

A slight vibration in the ground trembled up my legs. Not an earthquake, but a constant tremble like you feel near a heavy, running animal or the thunder of a waterfall.

"Wait," said Sean. "I do hear something."

"I told you!" I said.

The tunnel rose. Our lights flashed over a pile of broken rocks. And as we climbed over the breakdown of stones, noise rushed at us.

"Hey!" we said at the same time, "water!"

The tunnel ended suddenly, and we stood under an overhang of rock on the sandy edge of the stream. The water tumbled by, its voice deep, low, constant. It blustered flecks of water at us.

Sean put his finger in the edge of the water and tasted it. "Fresh water," he said. "And cold."

"What did you think it was? A hidden ocean?"

"I wondered if it was a hot spring, like at Uncle Hector's."

"How weird," I said. The voice of the stream echoed off the stone walls. "The San Gabriel River is almost dry, but here's all this water in the drought."

I put my hand in. It was too cold to swim in without wetsuits.

"Let's follow it upstream," said Sean. Our flash-lights showed us the sand along the water's edge, stretched up like a path. Probably because the mountains were so dry that even the underground river must be suffering.

We walked a long time. We changed flashlight batteries once because the beams were flickering. We ate some tortillas and drank the river water. It was perfect, clean and fresh. Then we rested again about five o'clock. I was yawning, wishing I could go to sleep for a while. If Sean hadn't had his watch, we'd never know what time it was, day or night. But our bodies would let us know when they were hungry and tired. We walked on.

"What if it rains and the underground stream fills up?" I said. I flashed my light around the cave. The ceiling was about a foot higher than our heads. I could imagine the water rolling down, filled to the ceiling, us torn under—

Yick. What a thing to think of.

"Not much chance of that. We're in the middle of a drought," said Sean.

"I know. It's just that I've been thinking of this cave as friendly. Like it was just for me. But now it seems scary."

"It *is* scary," said Sean. "It's a wild cave."

I felt dumb saying this, but I wanted to explain: "I had sort of thought that God was helping me by showing me this cave. You know, helping me to run away."

"Maybe he is. Maybe God is wild, like the cave."

"But if the cave's really dangerous—" I broke off, but kept thinking, *Why did God bring me to a dangerous place?* I wondered if I knew anything about God after all.

The sand was deep; we sank to our ankles in some spots. I stumbled over a chunk of rock, then kicked it into the river. The rock thunked in with a small splash.

I said, "But if this cave is really dangerous, then maybe God isn't the one who showed it to me after all." I shivered. Was it the enemy, then—Satan? Or was it nothing but a cave I'd found, not a gift from anybody, just the way I'd find a rock in the dirt? *Thunk.* Each of my thoughts dropped into my pool of turmoil with a heated splash.

If that was true, then maybe this running away business was wrong. *Thunk.*

So maybe I was giving Mama a hard time. And Francisco too. *Thunk.*

But they'd sold Burrito.

Sean stopped and gripped my shoulder with his free hand. "Reba, you want to know what I think?" he asked.

I swallowed and rolled my flashlight in my hand so the light spun like a star curving in deep space. "What?"

Sean said, "I think this cave is just here, no matter what. You say God wanted to show it to you, like a gift, as a place to run away to—I don't know, Reba. That's getting kind of strange. I mean, if there even *is* a God, why would he care?"

"He does care," I said. "He cares about the sparrow who is hungry. He cares about little stuff like a spider building her web and big stuff like people starving."

Sean snorted. "Then why *are* people starving?"

"Because other people are letting them! God isn't like this magic wand you wave to make stuff better."

Sean heaved a sigh and walked again along the river. "I don't know, Reba. It's all weird to me. It would be easier to believe that space aliens spawned us."

"Why did you run away with me then?" I asked.

"Because I didn't think you ought to be by yourself." He hesitated, then said fast, in a rough voice, "Do you think I want you to move away? You're my best friend, Reba."

I suddenly sat on the sand; my legs just popped out from under me. "You're my best friend, too, Sean," I said. And he really was. Why was life so complicated? Was Sean, like the cave, a gift from God? A wild cave, an unpredictable boy? Nothing typical about God, that was for sure.

With Sean in the cold sand next to me and the river running past, sounding like a flock of birds, we rested again. My legs ached from walking uphill.

Sean pointed his beam around the tunnel and over the laughing water.

"I wonder where the water really comes from," I said.

"Good question," said Sean. "I've been trying to imagine the outside of the mountain and compare it to what we've been seeing. It just doesn't match up. They're two different worlds."

Two worlds. The inner world and the outer world.

"Let's go on," I said. "I'm not tired anymore."

14

Crossing the River

We traveled beside the river for another hour or so. It seemed to be widening; now our flashlights barely shone across the waters.

"Dead end," said Sean suddenly.

We stopped. The sand, cold and heavy, trickled into the cuff of my sock and down my ankle. I shook my leg like a burro brushing away flies.

Our sandy beach path ended at a huge wall of rock that rose to the ceiling. The water rolled out from under the lip of the rock, thundering quietly like an upside-down waterfall. We'd never find out where the river came from, I guess. Maybe a scuba diver could figure it out, but no one else. Little triangles of water rippled near my feet. I flashed my light over the wet face of the slab of rock.

"Now what?" I asked.

We both flashed our lights around, studying things. Solid stone folded over us. Some of it was greenish-blue and glistening with moisture. Uncle Hector called it serpentine rock. Other rocks were white, pearly, veined in grey and glinting with fool's gold.

If only there was gold and treasure in this cave. Treasure to buy back the burros and the pack station. Treasure to make Mama's life and ours better. Would she have decided to marry Francisco if we'd had enough money?

"Look across there," said Sean. His light played across the stream and up on more rocks. "Shine your light here, too."

My light blended with his. Opposite the river was more stone, but one place looked different from the rest; a narrow shaft seemed to come down into the cavern, like the great stone walls had curled back.

"It looks like the pit I fell down," I said. For a minute I thought maybe we'd traveled in a great circle.

"Maybe it goes up to the surface," said Sean.

"Remember those things called blowholes?" I asked, thinking back to fourth grade again and the unit on national parks. "The water goes up them like geysers."

"One way to find out. Let's cross the river and look," he said.

I thought about his word, *cross*. Mama would sometimes say to us, "Don't make me cross!" Too bad the river wasn't like a cross animal to soothe, to make behave, to be eased out of its crossness for us to go across it safely.

Please, God, help us to cross the river safely. And I realized that was the root of all my prayers. To cross problems safely.

Sean rolled up his pant legs above his knees and took off his shoes and socks. He waded first into the water, holding his shoes over his head with one hand, the ever-present flashlight in the other. He yelped at the icy water.

At the edge of the roiling river I paused, my toes shocked by the cold water. Sean was in up to his knees when I waded in after him, the water so cold it burned. He was almost halfway across, the middle currents like a stream of grey paint sucking around him, when the rope tugged on my waist. The water was past his knees now, soaking the bottoms of his jeans. I hoped the water wasn't any deeper than that.

"Here goes," I called. He glanced back with a grin and pushed out farther as I plunged in. When I made it out to the middle, Sean climbed onto the slight bank and danced with cold, making the rope splash between us.

Since I wasn't as tall as him, the water crept higher on me, the middle of my thighs. Yick. The currents tugged at me, and the sand under my bare feet turned to softer mud; I sank into it to the tops of my feet.

Sean dropped his shoes and socks and waded back out. "Give me your hand," he said, probably because I was moving cautiously in the soft, uncertain footing.

"I'm okay," I said. "Don't worry."

He grinned and withdrew his hand. "So much for chivalry," he said, turning around—and suddenly sat down in the river.

I stopped, the water sucking around me, the rope taut. "What are you doing?" I squeaked. His flashlight sank; the cave was suddenly much darker.

Sean flailed and tried to get up, but he fell back in with a deep splash. The water soaked his shirt. He struggled up again and I moved towards him.

"Stay back," he gasped.

I was sure he was sinking in quicksand—or was it a monster sucking him under? I surged through the water and leaped onto the bank, my cold feet so numb that I hardly felt the solid ground. I dropped my shoes and set down our only flashlight so that the beam of light hit Sean.

He wasn't far from the edge, but he was up to his neck in the freezing water. He hung onto the rope, dragging me ankle deep into the water.

"Hold on! I'm going to pull!" I yelled. We played tug-of-war with the river.

Slowly I backed through the sand, hauling, my leg and arm muscles tightening. The rope stretched, then stopped, the strands tightening. I pulled as hard as I could, throwing my weight back.

With a sucking sound, Sean stood up from the river, then waded out onto the powdery sand, covered in thick mud. He fell to his knees.

"Like quicksand," he choked. "The water was starting to go into my mouth." Maybe because he weighed more than me he had sunk deeper. Or maybe he really had found a patch of quicksand. Behind him, the stirred-up mud looked like a mini La Brea tar pit.

"Are you okay?" I asked him.

He nodded and put his arms around himself. "I'm freezing, though."

I bet he was. My legs and feet were numb; his whole body must have been. He scraped at the mud on his jeans. I shivered, but Sean was much colder.

"Can you wear my jacket?" I asked. I helped him out of his shirt and jacket, then I reached into my pack for mine. His skin was puckered and purplish. "Maybe if you put this on."

It was way too small. I draped it over his shoulders. Better than wet clothes.

I fumbled with the rope knots and managed to untie us so I wouldn't keep tripping over the rope. Sean's teeth were chattering, his whole body beginning to shake.

"Come on," I said. "Let's move around. That'll warm us up."

We walked a path around the little beach. I put my arm around him. In this damp cave, he'd take forever to dry out. My fingers touched the matchbook in my jeans pocket. Still dry. But there was nothing to burn. Only sand and rock.

About the fiftieth time around the little sandy beach with our arms around each other, I remembered the pit. "Just a second," I said. I flashed my light up on rock. Solid granite and limestone. To go back the way we'd come would take several hours. If there was a faster way out, I wanted it. I kept flashing my beam over the rock wall that dropped down to the sandy beach.

Wait, there. My beam quivered on the subtle change in the rock, black on black.

"There it is," I said, and stood under it. My light penetrated a few feet into the darkness. "Let's try going up it," I suggested.

Sean didn't protest. This was kind of a harebrained idea, a gamble, but if it paid off, it would be worth it.

And if it didn't—then what?

I frowned, wondering how bad it was when someone's body got really cold with no way to get them warm again. Hypothermia, it was called. People could die from it. Maury had helped rescue hikers who had gotten lost, and cold, spending a night in the San Gabriel mountains. They often had to be hospitalized because they were so cold.

So now what, God? I thought. *Should we try to go up the shaft?* I chewed my lip. How would I know which was best? To go back or go up?

First I rubbed Sean's arms, trying to warm him up. *I* got warmer, but he didn't. I put on my shoes and socks, then put his on for him.

"I can't feel my toes," said Sean.

Why did I have to be the one to decide?

Out of my backpack I got the spare flashlight, the one with a crack in the case from my first fall in the cave, and handed it to Sean. I was glad I'd kept it. He examined it like he'd never seen a flashlight before. "Turn it on," I said patiently. He did and blinked at the light.

I decided in a rush. "We go up," I said, and herded Sean under the pit.

15
Looking
for the
Night-light

The way up to the bottom of the shaft was a little steep hill. I scrabbled for handholds in the rock and realized that my hands were torn. When did that happen? I had no idea. I held the flashlight in my teeth so I could use both hands on the rock. The shaft was narrow and steep; no easy way to climb it. I began to chimney up. I braced my back against the narrow pit of stone and inched up a foot.

I stopped, panting over the flashlight. Then, holding myself in place with one arm and my legs braced against the rock, I took the flashlight out of my mouth and shone it down. "Come on, Sean," I called. The light hit the top of his head; he was huddled in the sand.

"I'll wait here," he said, his voice thin.

"No!"

"I'm too tired to move."

"You *have* to come up here," I said. I didn't know a lot about hypothermia, but I did know I couldn't leave him behind, unmoving, wrapped in cold. Surely he'd warm up if he moved.

"Come on."

"No."

I gritted my teeth, then climbed down and pulled him up by his cold arm. "Get climbing," I commanded. When he didn't move, I shoved him.

"Hey," he said.

"Now, move!" I felt like a drill sergeant, but it worked. Sean started to move clumsily up the little hill toward the shaft.

Now if the pit really led outside.

We climbed vertically up the shaft for about ten feet, then fortunately it flattened out into a tunnel. Much easier.

I had to force Sean ahead of me. When I tried to lead, he would just stop and wouldn't follow. When he stopped in front of me, I'd yell at him to get moving, like I used to yell at the burros on a long trail. I'd tied the arms of my jacket around his neck and the arms of his wet jacket around his waist. I wasn't sure which was worse—wet clothes or no clothes.

The tunnel went on and on, sometimes wider,

sometimes taller so we could stand. And steadily, it went up and up, and I was glad for that.

Sometimes I thought that the darkness softened, as if a tiny night-light flickered ahead, but I couldn't tell where it came from. It was too diffused. Or maybe I was imagining it. All I could think was: *Get help.*

We crawled, bear-walked, crouched, and crawled some more. When my flashlight beam lit Sean's face, his blue lips scared me.

My fingers bled on the rock. I tried not to look down at them; my blood scared me. Mostly I just focused on moving ahead and pushing Sean before me.

After about an hour (Or was it a day? Sean's watch had stopped in the water.) the tunnel ended. Abruptly. Solid, white-veined rock blocked us. Not like the breakdown we'd crawled over, where pieces of stone had collapsed in a long-ago fall, but the-end-of-the-line, solid kind of rock.

I wanted to put down my head and howl.

"I gotta rest," said Sean. "I'm really tired."

So was I. But the idea of just giving up was repulsive. And resting, I feared, would be *permanent* giving up, at least for Sean.

But maybe if we rested just a minute. I wouldn't close my eyes. We put our arms around each other and shivered together. I blew into my hands, but that hardly warmed them.

We had to do something, but what?

Think, Reba, I commanded myself. But I didn't know what path to think down. Sean shivered in my arms. I thought: *The only thing darker than a cave must be a black hole in space. That place where light gets sucked in and never escapes.*

95

Light. If light is what I was looking for, I could find it better in the dark. I snapped off my light and Sean's.

"Hey," he protested.

"Just a minute. I want to see something."

He muttered something incoherent.

I blinked in the total darkness. But I had thought I'd seen a pale, pale light back down the tunnel. Now nothing.

"Come on," I said bleakly, without hope. I turned our lights back on and started back the way we'd come, the flashlight back in my teeth.

We crawled forever. I kept stopping and switching off the lights, peering into the blackness, but saw nothing except the dark.

The stream rumbled faintly, like the murmur of a distant conversation. Up ahead was the shaft we had crawled up. With a sigh, I snapped off both flashlights and stared into the dark until my eyeballs burned. Sean curled against my back, a slight warmth. He still shook with cold.

But this time it was different. After a few minutes for my eyes to adjust, the cave wasn't solid black anymore, but a softer, charcoal grey. So I *was* seeing light—if it wasn't my imagination. But where was the light coming from? It spattered like light rain, diffused and pale.

I snapped my light back on and searched the tunnel around the shaft that lead down to the river. Left, right, back, front, up. Up. The pit continued up. We'd gone off on one branch of it! I hadn't seen the rest of it because the rock bulged out, hiding the upper portion unless you craned your neck a certain way

"All right," I said. "We're climbing again." Sean didn't answer.

I scrambled back to him. "Let's go." I shook Sean. He was dozing, relaxed, his shivering lessening. Did I dare to leave him? No. I couldn't. We both had to keep moving.

"Wake up, Sean," I said and shook him hard. He muttered something. I think it was obscene, but I just kept shaking him until he lifted his head. "Let's go," I said and shoved at him until he stood.

Carefully, I climbed up the shaft first. I kicked at Sean until he started up, too. This section was narrower. The hard rock scraped my backbone until a trickle ran down it. Sean squirmed below me. He looked like a spider underneath me. What kind of web had I gotten us into?

We squirmed and gasped and wedged ourselves up on the rocks.

Finally Sean announced, "I'm stuck."

"Don't be a pansy," I snapped. But he wasn't. He was stuck.

I pulled on his arm, but I almost lost my balance. Great. I didn't want to fall on his head.

I peered up with the flashlight. The tunnel continued, and it didn't seem to get narrower. I thought I could keep going. If I could just find a way out. "Can you stay where you are for a minute?" I asked.

"Yeah, I'm wedged pretty good here," he said. "I think I'm a little warmer, too."

Somehow I doubted that. I climbed up farther.

The narrow shaft pinched my hips, my shoulders, and my legs. For once I was truly glad to be so skinny. Rock grated my skin as I wriggled and inched up. Alice in Wonderland fell *down* the rabbit hole, but how did she get back out? I couldn't remember. I snapped off my light, and the cave remained a soft dark, as if it were lit by a night-light.

Then, suddenly, the soft light blinked out, like a cloud over the moon. I hit a ledge, yet another turn in the shaft. I pulled myself onto it, glad for something horizontal, and lay panting. I reached up and felt the lip of the tunnel, still continuing up. Then I leaned out over the edge and called down, "Sean?"

No answer.

Panic swept over me like the river currents. He hadn't fallen, had he? Wouldn't I have heard him? "Sean?" I called again. I leaned farther off the ledge, flashing my light down. It glinted on his blonde head. "Oh, Sean!" I could have killed him for scaring me.

His slow, mumbled voice floated up, "Reba?"

"Geez, you scared me when you didn't answer. Are you okay?"

"Think so." His voice was slurred, slow, and thick, like Pio's one time when he came home late. "I'm a lot warmer now," he added.

That didn't sound good. I crawled as fast as I thought safe along the ledge, praying I'd see sudden holes before I plunged in. *So this is what a mole feels like*, I thought, scooting along. Only unlike a mole, I couldn't dig my way to the surface.

The light *had* to be filtering in from the outside. Where else would light be coming from?

At the end of the ledge I rolled onto my back and searched the ceiling with the beam. Solid rock glinted back. All the swear words I'd ever heard paraded through my mind. This wasn't fair! There had to be a way out.

So where was the light source? I snapped off my light and strained my eyes, searching for the opening. This was like a game, a puzzle, a maze. If only the stakes hadn't been so high. I rolled back over, snapped on my flashlight, and crawled slowly, peering up as I went. The ledge was long, much longer than the width of the shaft it jutted out from. I had trouble visualizing the cave and all its dimensions, but I thought I was crawling perpendicular to the pit Sean was hanging in. I couldn't be sure. And I thought the ground was straight above me. But I didn't know that for sure either.

Please, God, I prayed. *Help me find the way out.*

After all, God had drilled these tunnels. He could lead me to the opening. Couldn't he?

My flashlight beam stumbled over rough rock; there was a narrow, straw-like opening. I snapped off my light and peered into it. The night-light! Was this *it?* A hole only big enough to stick my little finger in?

16
The Wolverine's Secret

I rolled onto my back. I wanted to cry, but I was too exhausted. We'd have to go back the way we'd come. I should have done that in the first place. So I blew it. I didn't hear God's call after all.

I'd have to get Sean moving again. Then maybe if he felt warmer, I'd leave him and run back and get our supplies. I hoped I'd have the strength. Fatigue pulled at my legs already.

All the way back to the cave entrance. Back the way we'd come. I couldn't think of any other way out.

The light filtering down through the tiny straw-size hole was so faint; maybe it was winding a long way down through the rock, and that meant we still might have a long way to go to the surface anyway. Or maybe it was night outside.

Wearily, I rolled over to crawl back to Sean—and my hand brushed something soft, like fur. For a wild moment I thought of Burrito—as if a burro, even a baby burro, could fit into this tunnel, not to mention that burros and horses know instinctively that shadowy places are unsafe and will refuse to enter them. Under rocks and trees, mountain lions can jump onto their back, bite their spine, and kill them.

But the fur. I shone the light on the clump. The fur, snagged on an especially rough spot, was dense black with a few white hairs mixed in it. Then a rich, pungent, and familiar scent transported me back a few months to the time I was running and hiding from the bounty hunter. Running with my wild, dark shadow, the wolverine.

I picked up the thatch of fur. The wolverine had been here. His scent was old, not fresh. Why would he be deep in the cave? Did he use it as a burrow, a shelter? If so, then would he have traveled as far as Sean and I had, without light? How could he have climbed up the vertical shafts? Wolverines climb trees, but unless he had rock climbing equipment I doubted he could have climbed the smooth rock walls.

And that meant the wolverine came in here some other way. And I would find it.

I yelled for Sean. He answered sleepily. Frantically, I flashed the light along the rock, looking for the answer.

Please, God, for Sean's sake. Do you want him to die while he still doesn't even believe in you?

I hunted, crawling up and down the tunnel, poking into every crevice, every now and then yelling for Sean and holding my breath until he answered, fainter each time.

My head bumped into an overhang. I rubbed my scalp and peered around the lumpy ceiling. And saw it.

The wolverine entrance.

The hole up was as big around as me. More pungent fur clung to the rocks. The hole was almost like an optical illusion. A rock jutted out from one side, almost covering the hole. Above that rock, another one jutted from the other side of the shaft. So unless you were lined up just right, looking right where the two rocks almost met in the middle, you'd miss the hole.

And the light was faint; it was night, and the sky was soft grey with clouds.

I wondered: Should I go back right then and try to squeeze Sean up the shaft and out? We'd do better up on the surface than in the cave. We could build a fire, for one thing.

Maybe I'd first better see where we were.

I crawled up out of the cave.

To the surface. I took deep breaths, like I'd been swimming underwater for a long minute. The night breeze snatched at my hair.

Something stirred in the bushes. I slowly drew my legs out of the cave hole and stood. I half expected the wolverine to appear, but only the breeze rippled, shifting the chaparral, stirring the tall greasewood.

I squinted up through the framework of oak branches. Leo, the lion constellation, gleamed above me and I got my bearings. North. South. The cave exit faced east.

The curve of the mountains didn't particularly look familiar, but then it was too dark to sight mountain peaks. The wolverine's trail led away from the cave exit. If I followed it, it would eventually cross other, larger trails, trails I knew. Maybe I should follow it; if I was near any cabins, I could get help for Sean.

Or should I check on Sean first? Try to unstick him and get him up here? Build a fire and warm us up?

My feet made my decision for me. They broke into a jog, dropping down onto the path. I made a mental photograph of the cave exit.

That narrow trail led to a larger trail, and as I ran my legs and feet knew that trail. They ran automatically, like a dog long on a scent. Loping through the darkness, pushing aside barely seen branches, my mind finally caught up with my legs. This was the trail to Uncle Hector's. And I was nearly at his cabin.

Thank God, thank God.

I blasted down the trail now. His cabin rose dark against the sky. I jumped the stone wall—but no Rufus, his dog, to greet me.

Uncle Hector's Medicine Hat horse wasn't in the pasture. Could he be in the barn? My heart thudded with disappointment. Uncle Hector couldn't be gone. Not tonight of all nights.

I ran up to the cabin, shouting his name. When I flung opened the cabin door, the fireplace was cold, the cabin empty.

He hardly ever left his cabin, especially at night. After lighting a lamp, I ran through the cabin. I took two blankets from his bed. From his closet, a flannel shirt and a pair of jeans. I slipped into another flannel shirt for myself. In the kitchen, I grabbed more matches, filled a can with water after taking a long drink myself, then grabbed some crackers and a hunk of cheese.

I carefully shut the cabin door and ran as fast as I could back to the cave exit. Keeping the shirt and pants, I left the rest outside the cave and crawled back into the darkness.

It was harder going down. I climbed carefully, my leg muscles shaking. When I reached the long ledge, I paused to yell for Sean. He didn't answer.

"Sean!" I screamed it this time. Still nothing. If he had fallen—

No. He couldn't have fallen; he was wedged too tight. That was the problem. Trying to unstick him.

"Sean?" My voice didn't echo, just thudded off the close rock walls.

"Reba?"

Thank God. I nearly collapsed with relief at his thin voice. I clung to the rocks above him, looking down the pit. My flashlight beam caught his blonde hair and the curve of his glasses as he looked up.

"You took forever," he said, accusingly, his lips still blue. But I figured if he could be ticked off he couldn't be in such bad shape.

"I found a way out of here," I said. "We've got to get you up."

"I don't think I can move at all," he mumbled, his tongue tripping over the words. "I'm wedged in. Plus my muscles keep cramping. I'll fall if I try to move."

"But you have to," I said. "There's no other way."

What if we *couldn't* get him up? Should I bring the

blankets and water I'd taken from Uncle Hector's, gather firewood, and then haul it all down to the beach by the underground river and build a fire? After I got Sean warmed up, we could go out the regular way. But to do that, Sean would have to move back down. I wondered whether he was strong enough to do either. And right now he was a lot closer to the surface than to the river.

I'd made it up the tunnel; was Sean that much bigger than me? How could Sean shrink enough to squeeze through? Maybe I should tie the rope to something at the top here, to support him in case he slipped.

Suddenly, staring at Sean, my light flickering over him and his backpack, I knew the answer and started to laugh.

17

Aunt Kate and the Medicine Hat Horse

Are you crazy? What's so funny?" Sean demanded.

"Your backpack," I said, quickly sobering up. It wasn't that funny, really; I was just relieved. "Take off your backpack and you'll be able to squeeze up here."

The shock on his face was comical, but neither of us laughed. Carefully, slowly, bracing himself with his legs, he unshouldered the straps of his pack. He held the pack up to me, and I gripped it. Then I waited while he started to climb up, fighting his stiff, cold muscles. When he was an arm's length away, I reached down my hand. He took it without protesting, and I helped him up to the ledge.

The rest of the climb was easy. Dragging himself out of the cave, Sean stood as I had, drinking in the fresh air and gazing at the polished stars.

After he'd pulled on the flannel shirt, he made me turn around while he shucked off his damp pants and pulled on Uncle Hector's dry, too-big ones. After he changed I wrapped a blanket around his shoulders.

"I'll build us a fire," I said and handed him the cheese and crackers. He ate as I gathered stones for a crude circle, then dry sticks. Soon I had a small fire crackling cheerfully, and we shared the water. I let Sean eat as much of the cheese and crackers as he wanted before I took any. He was worse off than me.

"Are you warm?" I asked. In the firelight, it looked like his lips had pinked up, but maybe that was just the fire glow.

"Most of me," he said. "Sort of deep in my gut I feel cold. But maybe it's just habit and I'll get over it soon."

Habit. He was probably frozen to the core. I spread his wet clothes near the fire to dry. Sean had wrapped the blanket around himself twice so he looked like a little old Indian.

He quickly dozed off; soon he slid to the ground and slept. Gently I pulled his glasses off, folded them, and put them a safe distance from the fire.

I collected more sticks, built up the fire, and finally allowed myself to relax enough to sleep, dreaming of dark places and wondering if I'd ever see light again.

I woke to a crow's harsh alarm cry. The fire's ashes

smoldered. I sat up, rubbing my eyes. Sean was sprawled out, sleeping still.

A voice said, "I ought to kill you both."

Aunt Kate. She sat astride Uncle Hector's Medicine Hat horse, the white mare with a red splash between her ears. Sean sat up, reaching automatically for his glasses.

"Aunt Kate!" I said, glad to see her. Then I remembered I was supposed to have run away, forever. But I was still glad to see her.

Aunt Kate swung her leg over and dismounted. She tied the Medicine Hat horse to a bush and began to gather sticks for the fire. I jumped up and helped her.

"How did you find us?" asked Sean. He stayed wrapped up, and I wondered if he still felt that cold in his belly.

"I smelled smoke," said Kate, her dark eyes sparkling. "My nose is as good as a hound's."

We relit the fire and I huddled down around it, my stomach gnawing on itself.

"Breakfast anyone?" Kate asked and began to pull amazing things from the Medicine Hat horse's saddle pouches: bacon, a frying pan, pancake batter in a plastic tub, some instant coffee. She put a small tea kettle over the fire filled with water from her canteen. "Your mama sent all this," said Kate. "She figured you'd be hungry."

Mama. I wiped at my nose and didn't know what to say.

When the coffee was ready, we drank it down. It was perfectly awful tasting, but it certainly warmed me up. Then Sean and I ate greedily. I even licked my bowl clean.

Sean still acted a little spacey, like he had after he'd had the flu and a fever, but he said he was warm and full. I didn't want to think how he'd have been if we hadn't gotten out of the cave. I sent silent thanks up through the blueing sky.

"So," said Aunt Kate. "Gonna tell me anything?"

Sean and I looked warily at each other.

"How come you have Uncle Hector's horse?" asked Sean.

"He lent her to me. Now I ask: How come you have on Uncle Hector's clothes?" said Aunt Kate.

Sean made a face and pointed at me. "Ask her. I have no idea."

Kate turned to me with a level look. "Well?"

I chewed on my lower lip a minute, then said, "Sean needs to go to the hospital. He got seriously cold last night."

Kate leaned over to Sean. "Is that right?"

He shrugged. "I'm okay now."

I said, "He had hypothermia. Usually they take lost hikers to the hospital because of hypothermia."

"We need to go soon," said Kate. "Both your families are frantic, looking for you. Uncle Hector and I convinced them to wait until today to call the sheriff. I—well, I had a feeling that you two had run away."

I chewed my lip some more.

"Am I right?" asked Kate.

I could have her take Sean to the hospital and then I could go back into the cave. After all, I was the one who was running away, not Sean.

"So don't tell me," said Kate. She scrubbed the frying pan and our bowls with sand and repacked them in the Medicine Hat horse's saddle pouches. "Let's go, Sean," she said. She and Sean dumped dirt on the fire.

I stood, uncertain. Kate wouldn't force me, *couldn't* force me if I ran for the mountains. I had my supplies in the cave.

"Are you coming, Reba?" she asked me.

"Are they mad?" I asked.

"Your mama?"

I nodded.

"More scared," said Kate. "Sean's parents, too."

I guess that wasn't too hard to figure out. I drew in the dirt with my tennis shoe toe.

Kate untied the Medicine Hat horse, tightened the cinch, and gave Sean a leg up.

"If you're coming, can you walk?" asked Kate.

Walk? I could run. Run away.

But I didn't. I put my hand on the warm neck of the Medicine Hat horse.

Sean looked down at me, a question in his eyes, then a statement: *Don't do this because of me. I can go alone.*

I know, I tried to tell him. *I'm going back because I want to go back.*

Kate glanced at us both, then clucked to the horse. The sunlight spilled through the branches of the trees.

111

18
The
Return

On the way back my hands began to throb. There were little tears and cuts from the rough rocks; some of them began to trickle with blood.

Kate and I walked side by side, with Sean on the Medicine Hat horse in front of us. She saw me looking at my hands.

"What happened?" she asked again.

I took a deep breath. "Just a minute," I said and ran up beside the Medicine Hat horse. She swung her pale head over at me. Sean looked down. His eyes were hooded, but he smiled at me. "Do you mind if I tell her?" I whispered.

He shook his head. "No. It's your cave, anyhow."

Was it?

If I told, I wouldn't have a place to run to. But now I wasn't so sure I wanted to run away. Last night I wanted to, now I don't think I do. It would be great if I could run away sometimes, and then return. I needed a place to run to, a place to go and gather strength to fight things like moving, like Mama remarrying, like losing Burrito. And maybe it didn't have to be an actual place. Maybe it was something I could do inside of me.

I let Kate catch up with me. Sean and the Medicine Hat horse crossed the stream and climbed up onto the main trail to the canyon that led back to Chantry Flat.

I told Kate everything in a tumbling rush like a rain-swollen stream. She didn't say much, except to ask an occasional question. Sean jumped in a few times to explain something better.

"Do you want to see the cave now?" I asked when I had finished the running-away story.

Aunt Kate cast a longing look up the mountainside, but said, "No, we need to go back."

She was right. It was time to go back.

Mama and Maury were inside the ranger station behind the screen door. Mama had her back to us.

"Well, golly," said Maury, suddenly, catching sight of us. "Look who's here."

Mama threw open the door with a cry. The Medicine Hat horse shied, but Sean didn't fall off.

Mama stopped in front of me and glared. "I could just kill you, Reba," she said, repeating Kate's words.

Then she touched my face, my shoulder. Her whole face softened. "Come home, Reba. You too, Sean," she said. I followed her, not looking at the empty pasture. I thought I heard a burro snuffle, but I knew I couldn't have, and ran inside the house.

Pio was in the living room. When he saw me he said, "You are the biggest troublemaker on earth." But he smiled.

Miguel punched my arm. "I spent all night looking for you."

"Ah, you were glad to miss school," I said. Andres ran over and hugged me.

Mama handed Sean the phone and he dialed his number. He looked a little green. I turned away. It didn't seem proper to listen in.

After Kate put away the Medicine Hat horse, she let herself into the house. I sat on the couch.

"Hungry?" asked Mama.

I shook my head. Andres sat close beside me, the heat from his body a comfort.

"Where were you?" Mama asked.

Kate sat on the other side of me. I steeled myself, then found it wasn't so hard. I told Mama about the cave, about getting lost, about Sean falling into the water.

"Maybe we should take him to the hospital," said Mama. She and Kate discussed it a moment, then Mama jumped up to take the phone from Sean and talk to his parents.

I was quiet as Sean came in and sat on the floor. He leaned against a chair.

Mama seemed to think that Sean and I had stumbled into the cave and gotten carried away exploring. I could let her believe that. Sean and I stared solemnly at each other. I wondered what he was thinking and what his parents had said to him.

Kate yawned as Mama came back in. "Sean's parents will be here in a few minutes. They'll take him to his doctor's office and see if he should be admitted to the hospital."

"I'm okay," said Sean. "Just tired."

"Just in case," said Mama. Sean gave me a weary roll of the eyes and I almost smiled, but not quite.

"Where's Francisco?" asked Pio, suddenly. "And Uncle Hector?"

"Oh!" said Mama. Pio and Mama exchanged horrified looks. "They're still looking for Reba and Sean," she said. "I forgot about them. Miguel, run and tell Maury to ring the bell." She turned to me. "Our signal to let them know you'd been found."

The screen door banged hard and a few minutes later the big ranger bell clanged.

A burro brayed, and I turned questioningly to Mama.

"Oh!" said Kate this time. "I completely forgot. Come here, Reba." She grabbed my hand and pulled me up. Mama began to smile as we stepped outside.

Standing with his head hanging out of a stall window was Burrito.

19

Home for Good

I stood without breathing, staring at the little burro head, shocked and wondering if maybe I had hypothermia, too, and was seeing things.

"I followed the stock truck. I remembered a rest stop outside of L.A. I took a chance and they were there," Kate said. "I thought Aunt Kela would be furious if I brought him back, but I couldn't let them take Burrito. I figure I can board him at the stable where I used to ride. At first the driver wouldn't sell him back to me, but I told him a baby burro wouldn't be any good for anything for years yet, and finally he agreed and sold him back to me."

Mouth open, I could hardly take in her words. I walked slowly into the dim barn. Burrito rushed to the stall door and pushed on it. I unlatched the door, and he bolted out and flattened against me. Down I went, laughing and crying, tangled among his legs. He stepped on my hand and knocked me in the mouth with a knee, but I was so happy that I just hung onto his fuzzy neck.

Burrito. Burrito!

Kate was laughing in the shadows, watching our reunion. "Looks like I did the right thing, didn't I?"

I stood up. Burrito nibbled on my fingers. "How much did he cost? I'll pay you back—"

She waved her hand. "A gift. Save your money for his board fee. That'll keep you busy enough."

After I made sure Burrito was bedded down and given food, I went back to the house with Kate.

Sean's parents roared up the hill and ran into the house. They hugged Sean and said all the usual parent stuff: *How could you do this to us? Are you hurt? Are you sick?* Sean took it all calmly and hugged them back, telling them he was fine.

After a minute, I went up to his parents and said, "I'm really sorry. I'm the one who ran away, and Sean stayed with me because he was worried about me. So it was really my fault."

His mom frowned for a moment—I know she was thinking, *That Reba*—then glanced at Sean and said, "Thank you for apologizing. We'll take that into consideration when he's punished." My stomach knotted and they snatched Sean away.

But he waved out the back of the car window, unworried, as they drove off. He always said his mom's bark was worse than her bite.

Mama took my hand and we walked down to the top of the trail to wait for Francisco and Uncle Hector.

"I hope they heard the bell," Mama said. "If the wind was blowing the wrong way—"

"I can go look for them," I offered. Surprisingly, I wasn't tired any more. Maybe I was running on adrenaline. But it would probably hit me tomorrow.

Mama hesitated. Not that I could blame her.

"I won't run away, I promise," I said and suddenly knew that it was true.

Mama touched my arm. "They went up to North Fork and the Wilderness Area. We thought maybe you'd gone looking for the wolverine."

No, but I had learned another of his secrets.

Kate gave me the Medicine Hat horse to ride. I left Burrito because I knew he'd still be there when I returned. I rode back down the canyon to find them and ask them to come back with me. Even Francisco.